Zane

Macklins of Whiskey Bend, Book Five

Contemporary Western Romance

SHIRLEEN DAVIES

Book Series by Shirleen Davies

Historical Western Romances

Redemption Mountain
MacLarens of Fire Mountain Historical
MacLarens of Boundary Mountain

Romantic Suspense

Eternal Brethren Military Romantic Suspense
Peregrine Bay Romantic Suspense

Contemporary Western Romance

MacLarens of Fire Mountain Contemporary
Macklins of Whiskey Bend
The Cowboys of Whistle Rock Ranch

The best way to stay in touch is to subscribe to my newsletter. Go to my Website *www.shirleendavies.com* and fill in your email and name in the
Join My Newsletter boxes. That's it!

Avalanche Ranch Press, LLC
PO Box 12618
Prescott, AZ 86304

Book design and conversions by Joseph Murray at 3rdplanetpublishing.com

Cover design by Sweet 'n Spicy Designs

ISBN: 978-1-947680-82-1

I care about quality, so if you find something in error, please contact me via email at shirleen@shirleendavies.com

Description

What can a cowboy do when his past and present collide?

Zane Talbot is comfortable with his life. Whiskey Bend is perfect for the future he envisions. Managing stables owned by his friends, plus work on a new computer application, provides challenges, and propels him toward his goal of buying a ranch. What he doesn't need is a relationship with a former goodtime girl who takes up his time while stirring up ghosts from his past.

Sarah Hutchison has thrown aside her party girl lifestyle to focus on earning a teaching degree. Working forty hours a week at a nursing home and taking classes at the local community college leaves her little time for a social life. Not even with the handsome, taciturn cowboy working at her cousin's ranch.

But sometimes, life disrupts personal plans.

Thrown together by family and friends, Zane and Sarah fight their strong attraction with little success. Complicating their growing feelings is the appearance of a woman greatly resembling Zane's deceased fiancée.

As they increase their time together, other, more sinister actions are at work in the background.

The unanticipated dangers jeopardize the couple's tenuous connection, threatening those around them. As the dire implications become clear, will Zane be able to protect the woman he's come to love?

Zane, book five in the Macklins of Whiskey Bend Contemporary Western Romance series, is a stand-alone, full-length novel with an HEA and no cliffhanger.

Zane

Prologue

Bozeman, Montana

Staring straight ahead, fighting the urge to run, Zane Talbot tried to forget the events of the last few days. If only he could roll back time...

A wave of nausea assailed him. He couldn't roll back time any more than he could breathe life into Debbie Wilson.

The tie around his neck seemed to tighten. Zane wished the silk fabric could strangle the life from him, the same as the drunk driver had sucked the life from Debbie.

Running would be the coward's path. Yet he yearned to be anywhere but in the cemetery, surrounded by family and friends. Zane didn't want to believe he'd never see her again. The casket and quiet sob of Debbie's mother confirmed the reality of her death.

No one blamed him. His mind told him they were right. What was left of his heart insisted he may have been able to avoid the terrible accident, prevent the loss of the person who meant more to him than his own life. Debbie left this world, while Zane escaped with a few bruises and scratches. Why hadn't it been him?

He almost missed the soft hand on his arm. Looking into the anguished eyes of his mother, he knew, without doubt, the plans devised the night before were his one option for sanity.

"Zane? Do you want to put the rose on the casket?"

Rose? Glancing at his hand, he saw the single yellow rose. Nodding, he stepped forward. Sucking in a deep, shaky breath, he ignored the tears sliding down his cheeks.

"I'll always love you, Debbie. Always and forever." Bending, he placed the flower on the deeply polished mahogany wood.

Unable to deal with the pulsing pain, he straightened and strode away, ignoring the soft calls of his name. He had no place in mind, no safe haven where he could grieve in private. Debbie had always been his safe haven, the one person he could talk to about anything.

He'd called her his rock. She'd respond by saying he was her roller coaster. Then she'd laugh, slide up on her toes and press a kiss to his mouth. So many private jokes, shared memories. But not the future the two teenagers had so meticulously planned. That part of their lives had been torn away in a split second. One moment, she was holding his hand, laughing. The next...

Zane thought of his football scholarship to Montana State. Debbie had earned an academic scholarship to the same school. Both would go unused.

He thought of his decision. The one he had yet to share with his parents. They'd argue, he'd listen. In the end, his need to get away and start fresh won.

And if Zane was lucky, the years would pass, and the deep, overpowering ache in his heart would lessen.

Stopping at the far boundary of the cemetery, he dropped to his knees. A sob tore from his throat, then another, until his entire body shook. Glancing up at the clear, blue Montana sky, he blinked several times before uttering the one question he hadn't been able to ask.

"Why?"

Chapter One

Ten years later...

"Get after him, Ty." Zane smiled at the enthusiasm on the young boy's face. Boone Macklin's adopted son took to ranching the same as his father.

They practiced rounding up strays, the same as two previous Saturdays. Instead of steers, there were a dozen calves in the large, fenced pasture, all rushing around in a form of organized chaos. Tyler's rope swung over his head as he selected a specific calf. Letting go, the young boy watched the rope drift through the air, settling over the calve's neck.

"I did it!" He raised both arms in triumph, almost losing his grip on the rope.

"No celebrating until you finish," Zane shouted back, noticing Boone reining up beside him.

"He's doing real well. You're good at teaching him."

The men sat in silence for a spell, watching Tyler get off his horse to check the rope. Satisfied, he gently pulled it free, allowing the calf to rush away to join several others on the other side of the pasture.

"Helps he wants to be like his father. He might end up being the best of all of us." Zane cast a look upward into a clear, blue sky. After completing numerous assignments for the Army, then working for a company in Southern

California, he'd grown certain there were no skies to match those in Montana.

"Are you still planning to visit your folks?"

"Pop's operation has been delayed. Mom says to wait until it's rescheduled. She's right. I want to be there to help him recover from surgery. He's lost a good deal of weight, yet she's still too small to tend him the way he'll need."

"You know they're going to try and talk you into staying." Boone smiled as his son rode toward the swarm of calves to try again.

"Don't think so. They've made the decision to sell and move into town. I think they were waiting for me to tell them it was okay to sell. Pop took it hard. He always believed I'd come home to run the ranch after sowing my oats." Zane chuckled at the thought. "He never understood I didn't have any oats to sow. I just can't go back there to live."

Again, they fell silent. Both knew Zane's dating life had been almost non-existent since his fiancée died ten years earlier, a few months before both were to attend Montana State University. Boone and his brothers knew the story.

"It's been a while now."

Zane shot a look at his good friend, then shook his head. "Debbie was it for me, Boone. I have a good life here in Whiskey Bend. There's no reason to make any changes."

Boone understood. Some men loved once, filled their heart with the passion of one woman. When the relationship ended, they never reached out for love a second time. He figured Zane was one of those.

"Pop already has a property picked out. It's a place Mom has always loved, and it's for sale. I think he means to surprise her."

Boone's brows raised at this. "Do they have a buyer for the ranch?"

"Three offers without being listed. Word traveled fast once my parents made the decision. Other than helping them out after Pop's surgery and moving them to town, I won't be going back to Bozeman much. Being there is still hard for me."

"Did you see me?" Tyler's excited voice drew their attention to the young cowboy who rode toward them. "I roped three today!"

"We saw you, son. It won't be long before you're better than me and your uncles."

"And Kell and Zane," Tyler said in a voice so serious it was hard for the men not to laugh.

"No doubt in my mind. It won't take much to be better than Kell. But me? You'll need to work a little harder."

Pursing his lips, Tyler studied Zane before nodding. "I can do it."

"I'm sure you can, Ty." Unease rolled through Zane as he thought of the rest of the day. "Boone, I have a meeting in town. Any problem with me taking off now?"

"Nope. Do what you have to do. Will you be back for dinner?"

"I wouldn't miss one of Willow's meals. Not intentionally, at least. See you this evening."

Riding back to the barn, and continuing on his drive to town, Zane thought of the reason for the trip. Old memories crowded his mind, as they always did each time he allowed himself thoughts of Debbie.

After ten years, he could still picture her as she was before that fateful night. Wavy strawberry blonde hair, bright blue eyes always shining in interest, and a smile which could bring him to his knees.

Shaking off the painful reminders of the woman he'd never stopped loving, he focused on the reason for driving to town. Within days of accepting a medical discharge and leaving the Army, he'd established a scholarship in Debbie's name.

An exceptional student, who intended to study nursing, would be selected by the scholarship committee each year. Zane had established few criteria, other than the student had worked while in high school and had come from challenging circumstances.

The contributors to the scholarship were Zane and his parents, two teachers in the high school science department, and an anonymous donor who contributed every year. When the Macklins learned of the scholarship, they'd insisted on participating. None of them were wealthy. Still, the small group was able to award several thousand dollars each year. His parents always attended the award ceremonies. Zane had yet to make an appearance.

After their daughter's death, the Wilsons had disappeared. They'd left no message for him, and no forwarding address. He'd tried several times to locate them, even hiring a private investigator after leaving the Army. The woman had never been able to locate them. Their disappearance still nagged at him, but after ten years, he'd given up trying to find the couple and Debbie's younger brother.

Pulling into a parking space, he sat in the comfortable silence of his truck. He thought back on the last few years. Leaving the Army, he'd accepted a job with a tech company in Southern California, staying there until Kell and the Macklins encouraged him to return to Montana. It had been the right move.

The meeting today was with Kell's wife, Beth, and one of the law firm partners. They collected the donations for a deposit to a trust account in the scholarship's name. It was a formality, yet one which made everyone more comfortable.

He took the stairs to the top floor, sparing a cursory glance at the list of attorneys by the firm's entrance.

"Good afternoon, Mr. Talbot. I'll let Beth know you're here."

Offering a small smile to Alana, the longtime receptionist, he took up a post across the room. He didn't have to wait long before Beth Brooks appeared with a warm smile.

"Hi, Zane. Janet will join us in the small conference room." Opening the door, she stepped aside, motioning to the table. "Take any seat. Can I get you some coffee, water, or soda?"

"Nothing for me, Beth."

She chose the seat next to him, knowing he dreaded the discussion to come. "I know you've heard this before, but what you're doing will help some very deserving person."

"Thanks. I'm committed to keeping the scholarship alive. I've contacted the first recipient to graduate from college, asking for whatever support he can provide. You should've received a small amount from Robert Cheney. I told him all donations are acceptable."

"Any amount helps, and yes, we received fifty dollars from Robert. He enclosed a note saying he hopes to increase the amount with future donations."

"I'm happy with any amount prior recipients send." Gripping his hands in his lap, he felt a familiar chill race through him. The first year, he'd left the meeting as memories of Debbie flooded his mind. It took ten minutes to compose himself and return.

"Good afternoon, Mr. Talbot. It's good to see you again." Janet Chapman, a partner of the firm, shook his hand before sitting across from him. "This shouldn't take long."

She removed several papers from a folder, sliding them to Zane. "The first is an accounting of the funds received for this year's award. As you can see, it's ten percent larger than the previous year, due to five new donors."

Scanning the names, one brow rose. Debbie's two best friends since elementary school had sent money, as had three of his former teammates on the high school football team. Releasing a breath, a disbelieving lump grew in his throat.

"Do you recognize them?" Beth asked.

"Yes. It's, uh…more than I expected."

"They're people who miss Debbie and want to support the scholarship. This is one way they can keep her memory alive," Janet said, as if she'd experienced this in her own life.

Zane gave a slow nod, picking up the next piece of paper, he read through a short list of the students nominated for the award. "Two boys and a girl. That's a change."

Janet smiled at him. "More young men are entering nursing school."

Passing out individual files providing school records and resumes on each of the three, Janet allowed Zane and Beth several minutes to study the information. When finished, he set the files aside.

"They're all excellent candidates."

Beth closed the last file. "I believe this is the most difficult selection since we became involved."

Janet gave an almost imperceptible nod. "I agree. According to the original instructions, we do have the option of selecting more than one." She again noted the total, and the amount three recipients would receive. "We don't have to decide today. There is time to study the three over the weekend and reconvene early next week."

"Not necessary." Zane's quick response caused both women to stare at him. He took time to read each file once more before looking up. "My suggestion is to award sixty percent to this student, and split the remaining forty percent between the other two. That keeps the main award the same as the last few years, but also provides money to two other deserving students."

"Excellent idea." Janet glanced at Beth. "Are we all agreed?"

"We are. With your approval, I'll contact the school." Beth shot a look at Zane. "Unless you want to do it. I'm certain the principal would love to hear from you."

He didn't have to think long on the idea. "You go ahead. If we're finished..." Standing, he shook Janet's hand. "Thank you for doing such a wonderful job. I'm certain there are much bigger clients you could be working with."

"Not at all. The truth is, this is the kind of legal work I love. Will you be attending the scholarship ceremonies this year?"

A spike of pain pierced his chest. Giving a slow shake of his head, he sent a meaningful look at Beth. "Not this year. Maybe next time."

Gathering up the folders, Beth met him at the door. "I'll walk out with you." She faced him when they reached the elevator. "You do know you've never attended one of the ceremonies. Kell and I would be glad to go with you."

"I know, and appreciate the offer. It's just not time. Someday, but not this year."

"I understand. What are you doing for dinner on Saturday?"

"No plans."

"Good. You're having dinner with us after you and Kell get back from the horse auction. I'm making the potatoes you love so much."

"Bribery, Beth?"

"Darn straight. See you Saturday." Watching the elevator door close, she couldn't help thinking how a few seconds ten years earlier impacted so many lives.

Chapter Two

Tossing her books on the kitchen table, Sarah Mae Hutchison collapsed onto the closest chair while blowing out an exhausted breath. Her feet hurt, and head spun from another grueling day.

Long hours at the nursing home, followed by classes at the community college, took up all her free time. Nights and weekends were spent on homework, with the occasional evening with girlfriends or her cousin, Beth Brooks.

Sarah told herself earning a degree in teaching would be worth the long hours. Weeks like this one made her wonder.

Reaching into her purse, she snatched the ringing phone to see her cousin's name. Hesitating a few seconds, she answered.

"Hey, Beth. How are you doing?"

"Fine. I left a message earlier, but didn't hear back."

"I've been going all day. What's up?" Standing, Sarah removed a pitcher of tea from the refrigerator, filling a glass.

"If you don't have plans for Saturday, have dinner with us."

"Sounds wonderful. What can I bring?" Taking a sip of tea, Sarah already knew what Beth would say.

"You don't have to bring anything."

"Not even my chocolate cake? I'll even bring ice cream."

Beth chuckled, as Sarah knew she would. Her cousin couldn't resist the way too decadent cake. "If you have time. I know how busy you are with work and school."

"Not any busier than you."

Beth had made special arrangements with the law firm to work part-time while taking law classes in Missoula. She had almost two years left for her degree.

"Yes, but I have help. Kell's pretty good in the kitchen. I'll let you go. See you Saturday. We'll eat at six, but show up anytime."

"Thanks, Beth. See you Saturday."

Rummaging through the refrigerator, her mind wandered to Kell's good friend, Zane. Until recently, he'd been staying with Boone and Willow, giving the newlyweds privacy. Fifteen months after the wedding, Kell and Beth convinced him to move in with them. Sarah wondered if he'd be at the house on Saturday.

Zane was a good-looking man, and a loyal friend to Kell. They'd spent several years together as Army Rangers. Each would always have the other's back.

She didn't know why he intrigued her. Quiet to the point of sometimes being rude, he was the opposite of the more boisterous, outgoing men who attracted her. As far as she knew, Zane hadn't dated since arriving in Whiskey Bend.

Scoffing at the thought, she finished fixing a sandwich and sat down. Sarah hadn't dated in months. She'd spent considerable time with a local ranch hand, Brock Pattin, until he'd accepted a job in Wyoming. His leaving was inevitable. With work and classes, she'd had little time to miss him.

What sounded like an explosion had her running to the front door, drawing it open. She lived in a house owned by Thorn and Grace Macklin. Located in a good part of town, nothing much happened other than kids running through yards and teenagers playing loud music.

Walking across the front porch to the railing, she rested her hands on the top, taking a good look around. A block away, smoke rose.

"What do you think it is, Sarah?"

Shrugging, she glanced toward her elderly next door neighbor, who stood at the base of the porch steps. "I don't know, Mrs. Baumgardner. Seems to be coming from the block with the gas station."

"Oh, I hope not. That's where I get my gas."

Stifling a grin, she dashed down the steps. "I'm going to see what happened."

"Let me know what you find out."

"I will."

"And be careful."

Jogging the short distance to the corner, Sarah shouldn't have been surprised at the number of people gawking toward the source of the smoke. She gasped as her gaze landed on the flames coming from what had been a van. Someone had driven it into a gas pump. Her stomach turned over when she realized no one could've survived the crash.

She inched closer, feeling the intense heat from the flames. Firefighters were already on the scene, including the ambulance. The two EMTs were standing back, giving the firefighters room to do their job while making no attempt to get any closer.

Three men stood on the opposite corner from her. She recognized them as Sheriff Del Macklin, Kell, and Zane. Sarah wanted to join them, changing her mind when the fire marshal strode toward the three men, at the burning car.

Knowing there was nothing she could do, she took a few pictures with her phone, then headed home. There'd be time Saturday at dinner to discover what happened.

"The two of you saw what happened?" The fire marshal directed the question at Kell and Zane while pushing the recording application on his phone.

"The driver was ahead of us," Kell said. "The car cut across oncoming traffic, barely missing other vehicles. It swerved from side to side. I never saw brake lights before it plowed into the gas pump. The entire thing took no more than fifteen seconds."

"Only one person in the car?"

"I don't know. The driver was all I saw."

The fire marshal fiddled with his phone before holding it toward Zane. "What about you?"

"It was as Kell said. Except…" Zane's voice trailed off as he bit back a wince.

"Except what?"

Swallowing the bile in his throat, he met the marshal's gaze. "I'm pretty certain there was a passenger." Without another word, he turned on his heel, putting a good distance between himself and the others.

The scene reminded him too much of ten years earlier. Although he remembered little of the accident and trip to the hospital, the flames engulfing his truck would forever be etched on his brain.

"You all right?"

Hearing Kell's voice, he nodded. "Needed some fresh air."

"Are you still up for a beer or two at Wicked Waters?"

Zane didn't drink much other than an occasional beer. "Works for me."

"We can walk there from here."

Walking sounded real good. Striding out, he stuffed hands in his pockets, taking deep breaths to get the smell from his lungs.

"Hey, boys. Good to see you." Kull Kacey, the owner of Wicked Waters, came around the bar to shake their hands. "Do you know what's going on down the street?"

Kell answered for both of them. "A car plowed into a gas pump. They're evacuating the location and nearby buildings in case the entire site goes up."

"Geez. Must've been high on something." Scratching the back of his head, Kull pointed to an empty table. "Sit down. Beer?"

"The usual for each of us."

"Coming right up. If you don't mind, I'll join you for a bit."

Neither spoke as they stretched out their legs, letting the DJ music mask what they'd witnessed. It wasn't long before Kull returned with three bottles in his hand. Passing them out, he took a seat, resting his elbows on the table.

"The crazies are out tonight. I've had to call the deputies twice already, and it's only eight o'clock. They usually don't show themselves until at least eleven." Tipping back his bottle, Kull took a long pull. "Now we have the accident at the gas station."

Zane took three deep swallows of beer, setting down the bottle. Brows drawn together, Kull cocked his head at Zane, who nodded. Raising a hand for the bartender, three more bottles appeared.

"I heard from Thorn the breeding program is going strong."

"Breeding program and the boarding business." Kell took a short gulp of his second beer. "We're installing a large, covered arena, another round pen, and building with twenty stalls. With proper paperwork on file, we'll accept non-boarders who want to use the facilities on an hourly basis. We've gotten dozens of calls. No one close to Whiskey Bend offers a covered arena. It'll be a boon during the hot summer days and cold winter ones. You've met Cody, right?"

Kull nodded. "High school student who works for you."

"He's at the community college now, taking his general education classes. Bores the heck out of him. Cody works at the ranch thirty hours a week. He's already got a list of friends who are interested in coming on board once the boarding facilities are ready."

Zane tuned the conversation out as he listened to the hard beat of the music. On the dance floor were several older couples doing the two-step. They'd start at five and leave when the younger crowd appeared. The smiles on their faces touched something inside him.

He was tired of carrying Debbie's memory with him, unable to put her aside and move on. It had been too long since he felt anything for a woman. Much too long.

"Hey, boys. Anyone want to dance?" A tall, lithe woman with long chestnut hair, stood next to Zane, dangling a bottle of beer from two fingers.

Before he could stop himself, Zane stood, holding out his hand. Setting down the bottle, she threaded her fingers through his, allowing him to guide her to the dance floor.

Kell stared after him. "I'll be darned."

"I've never seen him dance."

Glancing at Kull, he shook his head. "Me either. Not once in the time he's been in Whiskey Bend."

"Well, it's about time he broke free of the past and embraced a future."

Kell's eyes widened. "You know of his past?"

"Enough of it to understand what we're seeing is unusual."

Their attention returned to the dance floor, where Zane and the woman were now moving to a jaunty country tune from a popular singer. Kell found himself smiling.

When Zane returned from escorting his dance partner to her table, he appeared more relaxed, as if a weight had been lifted from his shoulders. Taking his seat, Zane raised a hand for another beer.

"You sure, man?"

"Might as well. You're driving, right?" Resting an arm over the back of an empty chair, he flashed a lazy grin at Kell. When his friend continued to watch him, his face sobered. "It was a couple dances. No big deal."

Even as the words were spoken, Kell knew it was a lie. Truly enjoying a few minutes with a woman who made him laugh, had him forgetting about the past.

Picking up his beer, he tipped it toward Kell, then Kull.

Chapter Three

Sarah checked the time, rushing to place the chocolate cake in a carrier. Beth expected her early to help with the final preparations for dinner, and give them time to talk before Kell came in from working with the horses.

She found herself wondering again if Zane would be joining them. The thought had her mind going back to the accident at the gas station. A web search hadn't turned up the name of the driver, or much information other than the basics of the crash.

The gas station remained closed, yellow tape wrapped around the entire facility, with security guards protecting the site 24/7. The neighbors guessed it wouldn't reopen for weeks, forcing them to buy gas at the station across town. They also speculated the driver must've been a visitor, figuring no local would cross in front of approaching traffic. Sarah wasn't as sure.

Driving past the scene, she noticed nothing had changed other than the burned-out car was missing. Forcing herself not to dwell on the accident, she considered final exams. They were scheduled for the following week. Four finals in four days.

Turning onto the asphalt drive to the house, her gaze passed over the changes to the yard. Various sized flower beds dotted the open area between the road and house. It had taken her and Beth three Saturdays to complete the planting with a mix of perennials and evergreen shrubs.

An odd sense of envy surprised Sarah. She was happy for her cousin, glad Beth had met Kell and found love. Yet a strange trace of jealousy lodged in her chest.

Parking, she shook off the unwanted feelings. Gathering her purse and cake carrier, she headed to the door, smiling when it swung open.

"Right on time." Beth took the cake from Sarah's hand, ushering her toward the kitchen. "There isn't much to do. The salad needs to be assembled, the potatoes set under the broiler for a few minutes, and the rolls are ready to warm. Kell decided to grill steaks, so that's on him and Zane."

Zane. Why did the mention of him cause a pleasant fluttering in Sarah's stomach? She didn't want to delve too deep for the answer.

"I don't think we'll need them unless the boys' steaks are under sixteen ounces."

"If anything, they're larger. You know how they like their meat."

Chuckling, Sarah walked to the doors to the back deck, looking out. "It would be nice to eat outside."

"Works for me. So how are your classes going?"

"Great." She grinned. "Well, good anyway. Finals are coming up, then we have a week off. I can't wait to have a little time to myself."

Pulling the platter of steaks from the refrigerator, Beth seasoned them with what Kell set aside for her. "Still committed to going for your teaching credential?"

"Definitely. I'm tending toward elementary school. Maybe even kindergarten."

"Why not? You're great with kids. Tyler loves you."

A smile brightened Sarah's face. "Ty loves everyone."

"You also get along great with all his friends. I, for one, believe you're making a great choice."

"Anyone getting hungry in here?" Kell strode to his wife, kissing her soundly. "Glad you came tonight, Sarah. Give Zane and me ten minutes to clean up, then we'll get the barbeque going."

Zane appeared in the doorway, giving Sarah a brief nod before heading to his bedroom.

"They're right on time. What do you think of this for the salad dressing?" Beth handed her the electronic tablet. When her cousin didn't respond, she tried again. "Sarah? You okay?"

"What? Sorry. My mind was on something else." She wouldn't admit it was focused on Zane and how handsome he looked coming in from a day on the ranch. Unlike some, she didn't mind the smell of horse, hay, and the earth.

"Uh-huh." Beth's grin signaled she knew just who had caught Sarah's attention. "Take a look at this dressing recipe. I've never made it."

Sarah scanned the ingredients. "I think this would be great. How about I make it while you get the rest ready?"

"Perfect. I need to wipe down the table and chairs on the deck. You all right in here?"

Sarah glanced again at the recipe. "As long as I can find the ingredients."

"If not, let me know." The back door closed behind Beth.

Making the dressing, her thoughts lodged on Zane. She'd been around him many times since he came to Whiskey Bend. Lately, she'd been noticing him in a different way. What woman wouldn't notice the tall, muscled, and ruggedly handsome friend of Kell's? Since seeing him at the gas station accident, her fantasies had taken over, with him having a starring role in each one.

She should ask Beth about him, except doing so would spur her cousin's interest, and trigger questions Sarah wasn't ready to answer. Finding additional time for a relationship would be almost impossible. She chuckled at the ridiculous thought. Zane didn't do relationships or dating, as every single woman in Whiskey Bend already knew.

"Where's Beth?" Kell entered the kitchen, newly showered and shaved.

Sarah nodded toward the door. "Outside, cleaning the table and chairs. We'll be ready to eat as soon as you boys grill the steaks."

"Is that your homemade chocolate cake?" Lifting the carrier's top, Kell stole a swipe of frosting before Sarah could slap his hand away.

"Hey! Get away from the dessert."

"Maybe we should eat a slice before digging into our steaks." Zane's caramel smooth voice came from the doorway.

Turning, she held her real reaction to the man close, waving a hand in the air. "You can sure ask Beth. If she's okay with it, I won't object."

Holding her gaze for a moment, the hint of a smile tilted one side of his mouth before his head dipped toward the ground. Raising a hand, Zane shook his head.

"I believe I'll let it go. Eating a big slice afterward will be fine with me."

Turning back to the counter, she muttered loud enough for him and Kell to hear. "Good decision."

Chuckling, Kell grabbed the platter of steaks. "Probably best if we take positions outside, Zane."

"You won't hear me argue." Reaching over Sarah's shoulder, he plucked a cherry tomato from the salad bowl, popping it into his mouth.

Waving the paring knife in the air, Sarah glared at him, which he answered with a chuckle before following Kell outside.

Sucking in a slow breath, she forced herself to finish the salad. The last thing she wanted was for any of them to see her staring at Zane. Her life was messy enough without adding some strange infatuation to it.

"Tables and chairs are clean." Beth walked straight to the stove. "I'll pop the rolls into the oven. How are you coming with the salad?"

"Finished." Sarah tipped the bowl toward her. "The dressing recipe tastes great."

"Thought it would." Beth stared at her ringing phone on the counter, debating whether to ignore it. Giving in, she picked it up, seeing Del Macklin's name. Wondering what the sheriff wanted, she answered. "Evening, Del. Are you calling for Kell?"

"Afraid not, Beth. It's you I need to talk to."

"All right. What is it?"

She could hear Del clear his throat on the other end of the line. "You're aware of the crash at the gas station?"

"Isn't everyone?"

"Seems so. We've made a preliminary identification of the man driving."

An odd foreboding washed over her. "Who is he?" She heard Del's long intake of breath.

"Mick Vogel."

"What? No, it can't be." Her gaze darted to Sarah. "Not Mick." Closing her eyes, she sensed her cousin come up beside her.

"I know it's a shock. That's why I wanted to be the one to tell you."

Mick had taken an immediate liking to Beth when she arrived in Whiskey Bend. They'd gone out to lunch, met for coffee a few times, but nothing developed. He'd never given up, not even when it was obvious she had feelings for Kell. Still, they'd remained friends, with Mick offering her a position at his law firm. She'd turned him down.

"I spoke to his mother," Del continued. "She's not doing well."

"I never met her, but I know she and Mick were close." She touched a hand to her forehead. "Dead. It doesn't seem real. Do you have any idea what triggered the crash?"

"The medical examiner for the county believes he had a heart attack."

"A heart attack? That makes no sense. He wasn't old enough."

"Heart attacks aren't limited to older men and women. His father died in his forties from one. Anyway, the ME still has to confirm his theory. Thought you'd want to know."

"I appreciate the call, Del."

"I'll let you know the final outcome of the autopsy. That is, if you want to know."

"Yes, I would. Thanks again." Ending the call, she turned to stare outside, her face pale.

Sarah touched her arm. "What happened to Mick?"

"He was the man killed in the gas station crash. I can't quite believe it." Her skin remained a grayish color, her eyes glassy as she processed Del's message.

"What of the passenger?"

Turning toward her cousin, Beth shook her head. "I didn't think to ask." She scrubbed both hands down her face. "What a horrible accident."

Sarah stepped away, brows scrunching in thought. "What would cause a smart person to skip a lane of traffic to enter a gas station?"

"According to the medical examiner, Mick may have had a heart attack. He may have not meant to turn into the station."

"Steaks are ready, ladies." Kell stood in the open doorway to the patio, stepping inside when he saw the pain on his wife's face. "What is it?" He walked to her, Zane coming in behind him.

Beth explained before grabbing the rolls from the oven and placed each one in the basket. "He may have been a jerk much of the time, still..."

Wrapping her in his arms, Kell kissed the top of her head while whispering words of comfort.

Zane moved beside Sarah. "Did Del mention the passenger?"

"No, and Beth didn't think to ask. I believe Beth may have been one of only a handful of people Mick would call a friend. My understanding is his mother is quite ill, and his father died years ago. The entire accident doesn't make any sense to me."

Zane had to agree. He knew little about Mick other than the attorney had been interested in Beth before she met Kell. The man had never struck him as someone who took unconsidered risks, such as the erratic actions leading up to the accident. A heart attack could account for what happened. Still...

Stepping out of Kell's embrace, she picked up the basket of warm rolls. "Sarah, if you'll bring the salad, we can eat while the steaks are still hot."

Sending a meaningful look at Kell, who nodded in return, Zane lifted the bowl of salad before Sarah could grab it. "Why don't you head out with Beth? Make sure she's all right."

When she closed the door behind her, Zane turned toward Kell. "I don't like any of this."

"It's probably nothing other than what Del told Beth. A heart attack."

Zane gave a solemn nod. "I hope you're right."

Chapter Four

Zane adjusted his tie before slipping on his blazer. It had been over a week since the crash at the gas station, and there'd been no additional issues. He'd decided his concern about Mick's death was his overactive imagination. The worry experienced after Del's call had been unfounded, a product of his years as an Army Ranger.

He hadn't planned on attending Mick's funeral, deciding to accompany Kell and Beth in support of her. Somehow, planning the service had fallen to Beth, including the reception at their home afterward. If any of it bothered Kell, his friend had kept it to himself.

Sarah rode with them, sharing the extended cab of Kell's truck with Zane. No one spoke during the drive to the cemetery, yet Zane was extremely aware of her presence, the same as during Saturday's barbeque. There was no reason for it, and he found himself wishing for more space, more distance between them.

Relief gripped him when they reached their destination. Zane was the first to exit the truck, breathing in the warm air to clear his head. His relief hadn't lasted long. Sarah rounded the truck, slipping her arm through his to follow Kell and Beth to where several people already waited.

Squashing a sigh, he waved off the odd sensations rolling over him at her touch. It had been years since his body responded to a woman. Debbie was the last. He'd convinced himself never again would he develop feelings for someone else. Especially not the beautiful, yet flighty woman on his arm.

The thought gave him pause. Not once last weekend or today had he witnessed anything except a mature woman going about her tasks. So what if she partied with the best of them. A lot of men did the same. Daylight was reserved for their strong work ethic. At night, they relaxed, often having a drink or two, dancing, or just people watching. He mentally slapped himself, believing Sarah's actions were any different.

Zane's gaze moved about those in attendance, watching for anything out of the ordinary. "There aren't as many people as I expected."

"This is a town where people show up late for almost every event," Sarah answered in a soft voice. "My guess is those present are perhaps fifty percent of what will be the total." When he lifted a brow, she shrugged. "You'll see."

Taking seats next to Kell and Beth, Zane continued his vigilance of the growing crowd. He'd met Mick one time when the attorney was having dinner at Wicked Waters. It had been a short conversation, as Zane had been with Kell. Too short to form any opinion of the man.

A large group arrived, taking seats together. Most were in their twenties or thirties. All good-looking, dressed in sharp attire, the opposite of the common attire in Whiskey Bend of denim pants, t-shirts or plaid, long sleeved shirts.

Sarah inclined her head toward the group. "They're part of Mick's law firm. Attorneys, paralegals, and support staff."

"What will they do now?"

"I have no idea. Beth's employer is the most prestigious firm in town, working with longtime residents and ranchers. Mick marketed to new arrivals. The firm grew fast under his direction. It would be a shame if it closed."

A thirty-something woman about five-feet-six with ample curves and bleached blonde hair walked through the crowd. Several people stood to greet her. All of Mick's employees offered enthusiastic smiles, shaking her hand.

"That's Reverend Marie Farceur. She runs the High Rock Church."

Zane watched the woman stop at the head of the casket. "Never heard of it."

"It's relatively new. She attracts a younger crowd. Most are new arrivals in Whiskey Bend. I've never been, but some friends have heard her sermons. Farceur is apparently very entertaining." She smiled up at him while adjusting her hands in her lap.

Zane didn't often attend church, though most of his friends went to one of the local Protestant or Catholic churches. He couldn't recall the last time he'd gone with them.

"Farceur's services are on Wednesday night."

"Not on Sunday?"

"They don't have their own building, and no space was available on Sundays. I believe she holds services in an empty space at a strip mall south of town. The same place is used by a non-denominational church on Sundays. Rumor has it she and Mick had a thing going."

Before Zane could respond, Reverend Farceur began to speak. By the end of the service, Zane could see why she had a growing following. She had a conversational style, punctuated by sharp sentences meant to grasp the crowd's attention. Several times, her gaze landed on him and held.

Leaning closer, Sarah smiled while whispering near his ear. "You've caught Farceur's attention. Better watch out or she might snare you."

A shiver ran through him. She wasn't unattractive, but Zane had no intention of being snared by anyone. "Should I be scared?"

"Absolutely. Well, unless she's the kind of woman who interests you."

Farceur's voice raised for several poignant sentences before it lowered in closure. "On behalf of his family, thank you for attending. A reception will be held at the home of Kell and Beth Brooks." She rattled off their address before stepping back.

Seeing Beth and Kell stand, Sarah and Zane did the same. They walked to the truck in silence, climbing inside before Beth turned in her seat to look at Sarah.

"What did you think of Marie Farceur?"

"She does have a presence. Not sure I'd ever attend one of her services. I'm comfortable with our church."

Beth switched her attention to Zane. "What did you think?"

"She did her job. Beyond that, I'm fine kicking back with a cup of coffee and a good book on Sunday mornings."

Kell chuckled from where he sat in the driver's seat. "I'm with you, Zane. She didn't impress me enough to attend her Wednesday night services. Our pastor has a good message. I'll stick with him. Beth?"

"I'm good with our church. Change of subject. When we get home, I'll need all of you to help put out the food."

Zane listened with half an ear as Beth explained what needed to be done. Instead, his mind kept jumping to the woman sitting next to him. The same woman he once considered too flighty, too much a party girl to hold his interest.

That is, if he wanted any woman to hold his interest. Which he didn't.

"I don't believe we've met."

Zane winced at the familiar voice, in no mood to speak with Reverend Marie Farceur. Shifting to face her, he saw she held out her hand, which he took.

"I'm Marie Farceur. And you are?"

"Zane Talbot. A longtime friend of Kell Brooks." Sipping his beer, he leaned against the counter behind him.

"Ah, yes. Beth's husband. She is such a doll, taking charge of arranging the service and this reception. I understand they're still newlyweds."

"If you can be married almost two years and still be newlyweds."

"Of course you can. Why, I know couples who've been married five years and still consider themselves newlyweds. It's all in your mind."

"I suppose."

"You've never been married, Mr. Talbot?"

"No. I'm a committed bachelor. Have you been married?"

"Oh, yes. Three times."

Zane's brows rose. "You don't look old enough to have been married three times." He cringed the instant the words were out. "I mean…"

She held up a hand in understanding. "I'm thirty-four, Mr. Talbot. Each marriage was short-lived. Two years and three years. Two died. The third decided he loved someone else more than me. We divorced, and he married her within days." Shrugging, she sipped her wine.

"Ouch."

"Not really. I no longer loved him. I'm afraid my attention span doesn't lend itself to long-term, committed relationships. Still, I continue to try." Glancing around, she placed a hand on his arm, leaning closer. "Why don't you and I plan a time to meet for coffee? Get to know each other."

"Sorry, darling. I didn't mean to leave you for so long." Sarah rushed to him, taking his free hand in hers, getting on her toes to kiss his cheek. "I see you've met Marie."

"I sure have."

"Well, I'll leave you two alone. There are many other people I'd like to meet." The reverend flashed them a small smile before heading toward the patio.

Releasing his hand, she stepped away. "You looked as if you were about to pass out."

Zane smirked "Excuse me, but I never pass out. The woman surprised me is all."

"Shocked you is more like it."

Chuckling, he grinned. "That's true. She comes on pretty strong. Thanks for saving me before I said something embarrassing."

"Glad I was close enough to catch what was going on. You'll be on your own the next time." Patting his arm, Sarah left him standing alone as she headed to the counter of drinks to pour a diet soda.

Watching her leave, Zane felt an odd sense of loss. "This is ridiculous," he muttered to himself, unaware Kell stood a couple feet away.

"What's got you so stressed, man?"

"Who says I'm tense?"

Kell didn't try to suppress a grin. "You forget I've been with you on plenty of life/death situations, and you're as cool as they come. You've been ready to explode ever since we headed home from the cemetery." Taking a sip of beer, he waited. When it was clear Zane wasn't talking, he nudged him with his elbow. "You need to tell someone what's eating at you. Might as well be your Uncle Kell."

A burst of laughter tore from Zane's throat. "You aren't that much older than me."

"Two years, which counts. Now, talk."

Zane lowered his voice. "What do you think of Sarah?"

Kell's eyes widened before he masked his surprise. "Sarah, as in Beth's cousin?"

"The same."

Kell's gaze moved across the people in the house and those on the back deck. He found her talking to a couple of people from Mick's office.

"What do I think of her in what way?"

"Is she still a party girl with no clue as to what she wants to do?"

Scratching the back of his neck, Kell's mouth twisted. "Ever since she decided to become a teacher, she sticks to home. You know she works full-time at the nursing home and takes a full load of classes, right? Beth tells me she's getting good grades, and saves as much as possible toward her bachelor's degree. She's met Beth and me a few times at Wicked Waters, but always leaves early to study."

"I see."

"Well, I don't. What's going through that head of yours?"

Setting down his empty bottle of beer, his lips drew into a tight line. "When I figure it out, you'll be the first to know." Clasping Kell's shoulder, he headed out the door to join Sarah.

Kell stared after him in disbelief. "Well, I'll be darned."

Chapter Five

Sarah almost danced around the kitchen on Sunday afternoon as she put the finishing touches on the still warm chocolate lava cakes. Her supervisor at the nursing home would turn sixty the following day, and Sarah was determined to make it the woman's best birthday ever.

Other than Beth and Kell, her boss was the one other person who supported her decision to earn a teaching degree. Without the woman's backing, Sarah never would've been able to work and attend classes.

Satisfied with the platter of cakes, she covered them before setting the chocolate confections in the refrigerator. She made a mental note to make them the next time Beth invited her to dinner.

Her mouth spread into a tight line as she thought about the previous day. The service for Mick had been sobering, the same as any memorial for someone who died unexpectedly. The reception afterward had been the opposite. Friends and colleagues remembered him through stories, accompanied by toasts and laughter.

Zane had never spoken to her so much, asking questions and showing genuine interest in her classes. He'd surprised her by answering a few questions about himself. She'd hoped he'd suggest they meet at Wicked Waters or somewhere else before she resumed classes, but he hadn't. It was for the best.

She folded her apron as a soft knock sounded on the front door. Her neighbor had called earlier, asking to borrow a hammer for a picture she intended to hang. The request worried Sarah a little, as the elderly woman used a walker and couldn't be more than four-feet-ten.

Expecting to see the woman, she pulled the door open, she froze. It wasn't her elderly neighbor. Zane stood with his hands in his pockets.

"Afternoon, Sarah."

"Zane. What a nice surprise. Please, come inside. Would you like a beer or coffee or…"

Drawing a hand from his pocket, he held it up. "Actually, I was hoping you might have time to go to the park."

"Oh, that's right. The Sunday summer concerts start today." She stared at him a moment before the reason for his visit sunk in. "You're asking me to go with you?"

Looking down at the floor, he again stuffed both hands in his pockets. "I know it's late notice. I'll understand if you have other plans." She began shaking her head before he finished the sentence, causing both to laugh.

"No other plans. Let me get a jacket. Do you have chairs or a blanket?"

"I, uh…didn't think about them."

"No worries. I'll grab a couple chairs." Dashing to the back deck off her bedroom, she wiped down the folding chairs. Turning to head back inside, she stopped. Zane stood in the doorway of her bedroom, looking around.

"Thought I could carry them. You have a nice place here."

"Thanks. It belongs to Thorn and Grace. I'm lucky they offered to rent it to me."

"I was over at their place helping to cut down a dead tree. She mentioned you were staying here. My impression was they're real glad to have you." Taking the chairs from her hands, he headed back down the hall.

"I'm glad, because I plan to stay here until I graduate. Maybe longer if they're good with it. Should I grab waters?"

"Sure."

Pulling out a small, soft-sided cooler from under the sink, she added several bottles of water and a few plastic ice blocks.

"Something smells great." Taking the cooler from her hand, Zane slung it over a shoulder.

"Lava cakes. I made some for my supervisor at work. It's her birthday tomorrow."

"Right. The lady who talked the nursing home manager into changing your work schedule to attend school."

Sarah stopped in the process of picking up her purse. "You remembered."

A mischievous grin tugged at his lips. "Yeah. Sometimes, I surprise myself." Chuckling, he headed out the front door.

Watching as he set the chairs and cooler in the extended cab of his truck, Sarah couldn't believe Zane had invited her to the concert. He'd given no hint the day before. It must've been an idea after remembering the concert. However it happened, she was eager to spend time with him.

Any awkwardness Zane expected never came. Being with Sarah was effortless. She spoke when she had something to say, not talking to fill the quiet. He'd grown accustomed to hours of quiet time when recovering from wounds sustained during his last operation while an Army Ranger. Sarah seemed to understand this.

"May we join you?" Del Macklin stood next to his pregnant wife, Amy, holding chairs and a blanket.

Jumping up, Zane shook Del's hand before accepting a hug from Amy. "Wherever you want." He took the chair from her. "Let me help."

Sarah took the blanket from Del, spreading it out next to theirs. "It's good to see you. How are you feeling?"

Smiling, she patted her ample stomach. "Fat. Tired. Ready to bring the baby into the world." Lowering herself into the chair, Amy let out a relieved breath. "This is Del's first day off since the accident at the gas station. He's been working around the clock to wrap everything up."

"It's a strange situation."

Amy nodded while straightening her top. "That it is. Mick was so young to have a heart attack."

"Did they identify the passenger?"

"It was a woman from Missoula. Mick's assistant said he'd been dating her for a while. She was also an attorney. Del told me she handled criminal law cases." Glancing around, she looked at her husband. "Could you get me something?"

Cocking a brow, Del bent down beside her. "Something?"

"A sandwich, ice cream, funnel cake...doesn't matter. Oh, and one of those orange drinks."

"What about you, Sarah? And don't tell me you're not hungry. I can see it in your eyes."

Grinning, she held out her hands. "You're right. Whatever you get Amy is fine for me."

Straightening, Del motioned to Zane. "Come on. You can help carry."

They moved through the growing crowd on the lawn, Del stopping a few times to talk with people he knew. Veering toward the food booths, Del lowered his voice.

"I love my job, but there are times I'd like a private day with Amy. The longer I'm sheriff, the less privacy is available."

"You could quit. Do something else."

Del returned a woman's wave. "And do what?"

"Ranching. You already own a full share, and Boone is always needing help."

"Amy and I've discussed it. I'm not sure the ranch can support two families. Not yet."

Approaching the food booths, Zane placed a hand on Del's shoulder, stopping them. "You're a fine sheriff.

People respect you. Set some boundaries with your deputies. And get a private phone just for family and close friends." Zane dropped his hand, looking at the line of people at each booth.

"Sounds easy when you put it that way."

Zane shrugged, getting in the line for deli sandwiches, with Del beside him. He started to respond when a woman in another line caught his attention. She had her face turned away from him, yet her movements reminded him of someone he knew.

It was subtle. The way she pushed hair from her face with long, slender fingers. How she crossed her arms in impatience before leaving the line and disappearing in the crowd.

"Zane. You all right?" Del's voice jarred him from the woman.

"Yeah. Thought I recognized someone, but it was nothing." The woman forgotten, he ordered food and drinks, ready for a casual evening with Sarah.

"So you and Zane, huh?"

Sarah shook her head, wishing Amy was right. "Not really. He decided to come to the concert and thought of me. It was a last minute thing."

"He sure is a nice guy. If he ever comes to terms with his past, some woman's going to be very lucky." Reaching down, Amy massaged both calves before relaxing back into the chair.

"I've only heard the basics from Beth. Zane's girlfriend died in a car accident."

"She was his fiancée, and it was a long time ago."

Sarah shifted in her chair toward Amy. "How long?"

"About ten years, I think."

"Ten?"

Amy nodded. "Zane told us about it one night at the ranch when the entire family was around. He'd probably tell you what happened if you asked."

Sarah thought about it, dismissing the idea. If Zane wanted to share the details with her, she'd listen. She was saved from responding when she spotted the men. "There they are."

Zane and Del approached, their hands full of food. Sitting straighter, Amy reached behind her to massage her lower back. "You boys are the best."

"I've been telling you that for years, sweetheart." Del bent to kiss his wife. "What do you want first, the turkey sandwich or ice cream?"

Amy's features became serious. "Ice cream."

Del grinned at Zane. "You owe me five bucks."

"You bet on what I'd want first?" Amy spooned a large bite of frozen goodness into her mouth. "Oh. This is so good."

Chuckling, Zane pulled a five from his wallet. "I was certain you'd go for the healthy choice first."

Licking a dab of ice cream from the corner of her mouth, Amy shook her head. "Well, you were wrong."

The grin never left Zane's face as his attention moved to Sarah. "Appears so. What would you like?"

She'd been watching him, studying the subtle changes in his features. Numerous questions rolled through her mind. Questions about his past, the fiancée who'd died, why he was living in Whiskey Bend instead of Bozeman.

Sarah had been open about putting her partying ways behind her to pursue a teaching degree. She'd talked of her plans for the future, and the challenge of working full-time while taking classes. Recalling their few conversations, it became clear Zane had shared little about himself.

"Sarah?"

She blinked, focusing on the food in his hands. "A sandwich would be great."

Unwrapping it, Sarah took a bite, chewing as she considered private pasts and personal secrets. She found herself wondering if she'd ever have the courage to ask Zane about his.

Chapter Six

"Each box stall has an attached outdoor pen for your horses. They include automatic watering units and a locker for tack. We feed mornings and late afternoons, with the hay of your choice. Supplements can be added, and there's no fee if you prepackage them for us."

Zane continued to list the amenities as he showed a couple the facilities. He believed they were already planning to board their two quarter horses with them. They just needed one more tour before signing the agreement. They'd be their third boarders. The first was a longtime friend of the Macklins, with two grown mules, and the second a doctor and his wife who'd recently relocated from Denver. Both were eager to provide positive feedback on the facility.

"Do you have any questions?" He knew the couple would come up with one or two before finalizing their decision.

"Tell us again about the trails," the wife asked.

"We have several miles of private trails on the property, plus direct access to the Bitterroot National Park and Selway-Bitterroot Wilderness."

Zane thought of Sarah, wondering if she'd enjoy a Sunday ride. He shoved the idea aside. Why was he thinking about her during a tour? Why was he thinking of her at all?

"Plus, we have the trailer, sweetheart." The husband placed an arm around his wife. "We can go wherever we want."

He answered another question as the three walked to the office. After reviewing the agreement, they signed, with a request to bring their horses over by the end of the week. Accompanying the couple to their car, Zane returned to the office.

He had another potential boarder coming by after lunch, giving him enough time to complete a small pile of paperwork before getting something to eat. Picking up the first file, he started to review it, finding he had to begin again after the first page. He couldn't remember anything he'd read.

It wasn't as easy as he'd imagined to keep his mind off Sarah. A week had passed since the concert. He'd thought of her several times each of the days in between, fighting the urge to call her. Rubbing a finger across his brow didn't help Zane remember why he fought seeing her.

He grabbed his phone before he could change his mind and made the call. It took four rings before he remembered her tight schedule. Hesitating a moment at the beep, he cleared his throat.

"Sarah, it's Zane. Do you have time to grab dinner on Friday or Saturday? Let me know." Leaving his number, he experienced a wave of panic before ending the call.

It had been over ten years since he'd asked a woman out on a date. Did asking your fiancée qualify as a date? He didn't have an answer.

The years since had included a few hookups, all unsatisfying, further solidifying his inclination to hang out with his buddies. He didn't know why Sarah changed his feelings.

Over his lifetime, Zane had met dozens of women he'd considered stunning. Sarah was pretty in a small town girl sort of way. Nothing that would normally push his buttons. What did resonate with him was her focus on goals, her work ethic, and determination to become a teacher.

There were no pretenses with her. What he and everyone else saw was pure, undistilled Sarah. Down to earth, minimal makeup, jeans, and t-shirts. Her genuine smile and the sparkle in her eyes flooded him with warmth. All he wanted was to enjoy her company for as long as she'd allow, or until he lost interest and moved on.

A soft knock preceded the office door opening. The woman who entered could've been anywhere between twenty-five and forty. Tall and lithe, her long, dark brown hair was pulled back in a sleek ponytail.

"Mr. Talbot?"

Standing, he walked around the desk, extending his hand. "That's me. And you are?"

Taking his hand, she inched closer. "Rona Kessler. I called yesterday about taking a tour of your facilities." Her hand lingered a moment in his before she let go. "I'm early."

"No problem. I have time now to show you around."

"Thank you, Mr. Talbot."

"Call me Zane. We'll start at the first barn on your right." He motioned for her to precede him outside. "Do you have one horse?"

"Four, actually. Two quarter horses, an Arabian, and a Thoroughbred. I brought them out from Texas."

"That's where you're from?" He didn't hear any regional inflection in her voice.

"Born and raised outside Dallas. I returned after college back east. My family bought the Darling place a few miles from here."

Zane knew of the large ranch, and how it had been involved in an estate war since the couple who owned it died in a plane crash. "Why don't you keep the horses there?"

"The property requires substantial work before I can move in. I need a place for my horses until the ranch is ready and workers have been hired. You wouldn't be interested in a new position, would you?"

"I'm good here. The fact is, we're looking for ranch hands, too."

"Figures." She quieted as they entered the barn. Her gaze moved over the stalls and open area before connecting with Zane. "This is beautiful. I understand you plan on building three or four barns in all."

"Two to start. We have plenty of land for expansion. There's a large, covered arena, round pen, and hot walker. We're completing an outdoor arena and a separate obstacle course for those interested in dressage. Would you like to see them?"

"I would."

The remaining part of the tour took another thirty minutes. Watching her slide into a sleek sports car with the signed agreement in her hand, a grin tugged at his mouth. No doubt Rona was a woman any man would find attractive. He found her enticing, and for a moment, considered asking her to dinner.

Then an image of Sarah materialized. Warmth spread through him, accompanied by a sense of peace.

His phone vibrated in his pocket. Dragging it out, the grin became a full smile. "Hey, Sarah."

"Hi. I don't have much time, but dinner this weekend sounds great. If it's okay with you, Saturday is better than Friday. We can meet wherever you want."

A frown etched his face before vanishing. "How about I swing by and pick you up at seven?" When she didn't respond right away, he wondered if he'd pushed too hard.

"That sounds fine to me. Casual, right?"

"Definitely. I'd better get going. I'll see you Saturday."

"Looking forward to it, Zane. Have a good week."

"You, too, Sarah."

Beth waved to Sarah across the expanse of the small downtown bistro. They'd agreed to meet for a quick dinner before both attended evening classes.

"Thanks for meeting me." Sarah bent down, bussing a kiss across Beth's cheek. "I know you don't have much time."

"I'm in better shape than you. My class is online, so I can watch it anywhere. Yours is at the college." Beth nodded to the wine glass. "I ordered us Chardonnay and salads to save time." Waiting until Sarah put her purse and light jacket on a chair, Beth leaned toward her. "So, what's going on?"

Edging her chair closer to the table, Sarah glanced around one of her favorite restaurants before focusing on her cousin. "I don't know. It's silly really."

"What's silly?" Picking up her fork, Beth lifted a mouthful of salad.

Swallowing a sip of wine, she hesitated a moment before blurting out what was on her mind. "Zane asked me to dinner on Saturday."

Beth's eyes widened slightly as she set down her fork. "As in a date?"

"Well, I don't know. He left me a message asking if I had time for dinner on Friday or Saturday. I listened to it several times before working up the courage to call him back. He never mentioned it being a date. You know him better than me. What do you think?"

Lifting her glass of wine, Beth took a small sip as she thought about the Zane she'd come to know. "Are you meeting him at the restaurant?"

"He's picking me up. I'm sure it's more convenient for him."

"Maybe." Beth tapped a finger against her lips. "Zane is different from most men. He doesn't do anything without a lot of thought. I'm not sure he's been on an actual date since Debbie died."

"His fiancée?"

"Right. In all the time he's been in Whiskey Bend, I can't recall a single time he's even had a hookup. Of course, that's something he'd tell Kell. Not me." Lifting a piece of flatbread, she took a bite. "We don't talk much about Zane's personal life, other than saying how great it would be for him to find someone. He's such a terrific guy."

Sarah picked at her salad, mulling over Beth's words. She thought him a terrific guy, too, which is one reason she had to be careful about not reading too much into him asking her to dinner.

"He's the kind of man a woman could fall for without realizing the extent of her feelings."

Beth gave an almost imperceptible nod. "I hear you. The thing with Zane is he doesn't know how attractive he is. I'd guess there are a dozen single women in town who'd jump at the chance to have dinner with him."

Sarah believed the number was much higher. "He's a catch. Smart, great looking, with a good job. I can understand why so many women would jump at the chance to go out with him."

"Plus, he's got a bunch of money stashed into a brokerage account. Zane and Kell have a friend from their Ranger unit who's an investment advisor. Kell says he's real sharp. The guy has quadrupled the money they've given him since leaving the service. The three Macklin brothers are using him now."

When Sarah didn't respond, Beth placed a hand on her arm. "I know the money isn't the reason you like him. I'm just saying he's not a hundred percent reliant on his work at the ranch. "Oh, and he developed a computer game, which was sold to one of the big gaming companies. Well, the licensing rights, anyway. He's got a nice check coming in each month he adds to the brokerage account."

"He must be even smarter than I imagined." Much smarter than her, Sarah thought, as she swallowed a bite of salad.

Beth noticed how her cousin's mouth drew into a tight line, the sparkle in her eyes fading. "If you're thinking he's out of your league, you are dead wrong, Sarah Mae. You are every bit as smart as him. You work hard, have specific goals, and a big heart. Any man would be lucky to catch you."

Twirling the glass of wine between her thumb and fingers, a wry grin appeared on Sarah's face. "Well, I'm not trying to catch anyone. All I want is someone to spend time with. It'll be a long time before I'm ready to consider anything more."

"Well, then, you and Zane are perfect for each other. My guess is he's looking for the same."

Walking the short distance back to her house, Sarah found herself thinking about Beth's words. Maybe they were right for each other. Not so much right in the long-term, but good for right now.

All she had to do was keep that in mind, and not allow herself to fall for one of Whiskey Bend's most eligible bachelors.

Chapter Seven

Checking herself in the mirror, Sarah wrinkled her nose before slipping out of the blue blouse and tossing it onto the bed. Grabbing a red cotton blouse, she put it on, tying it at the waist. Paired with tight jeans and black sandals, Sarah felt she looked pretty good.

Satisfied, she picked up a black denim jacket and headed to the living room. She checked the time. Zane would be arriving within minutes.

Her gaze traversed the kitchen, landing on the cup of chamomile tea she'd made to help settle her uneasy stomach. Swallowing a large gulp of the tepid liquid, she choked as a knock sounded on the front door.

Coughing to clear her throat, she lifted a tissue from the box, dabbing at her eyes. Halting at the door, she inhaled a fortifying breath. Drawing the door open, her breath caught at the sight of Zane.

A black t-shirt molded over his chest, emphasizing rolling muscles. Black jeans hugged his legs and hips. His black boots were shined to a glossy gleam. Finally, a gray suede jacket was slung over one broad shoulder. The look would've been perfect on a GQ cover.

"Wow. You look amazing." She glanced down at her older jeans, discount store blouse and sandals. "Should I change?"

"Not for me." His appreciative gaze moved over her as a smile crept across his face.

Feeling herself blush, she stepped aside. "Did you want a beer or wine before we go?"

"I'm good. Are you ready?" He held out a hand to take her jacket.

"Yep. Where are we going?"

"Do you like surprises?"

She shot him a brilliant smile. "Love them! I'll just sit back and enjoy the ride."

"That's the first surprise." He didn't let go of her hand when they reached the sidewalk.

"Oh?"

"We won't be riding. We'll be walking."

Her mind ticked off restaurants which served dinner and were within walking distance of her house. There were several, and any would be fine with her. When they turned a corner taking them away from the business district, she glanced up at him.

"Um...there aren't any restaurants in this direction."

"Another surprise. There's a new place we'll be trying."

"Not a chance. I would've heard about it."

"Sarah, you're so busy with work and school, you haven't kept up with all the changes. This is my attempt to keep you updated."

A throaty laugh was her response. "All right, Zane. Show me what I don't know."

Turning at the next block, she spotted an older house the owners had remodeled to mimic an English cottage. With the summer sun slowly setting, she noticed twinkling lights, a new patio surrounded by flowering bushes, and the original wraparound porch dotted with tables and potted plants. They stopped in front of a white picket gate.

"Oh, my gosh. Has this been turned into a restaurant?"

Zane looked down at her. "It has. According to Beth, the food is great."

"How did I not know about this?"

"You're either working or studying. You need reasons to get out and enjoy what's around you. I'm determined to make that happen."

Disappointment churned in her stomach. Sarah had been nursing a small thread of hope Zane kept coming around because he had a genuine interest in her. The reality became clear. He saw her as a pal he could call without worrying about their friendship developing into something more.

Sarah had two choices. Stop responding when he called, or accept the friendship he offered.

She felt his hands rest on her waist before his soft breath wafted across her neck. "What do you say we get a table?"

Surprised at the intimacy of his touch, she moved away, turning to look at him. "A table sounds perfect."

Reaching out, he took her hand, his eyes crinkling with amusement. "I don't bite, you know."

"I'm not so sure," she mumbled, causing him to throw back his head in laughter.

They opted for a table on the porch facing a garden filled with ripening vegetables. Sarah found herself studying each plant while wondering which ones she could grow with her limited time. The house she rented from Thorn and Grace had a wonderful back yard, perfect for a garden.

"What would you like to drink, Sarah?"

Tearing her attention away from her envy of the beautiful yard, she looked up at their waitress. "Chardonnay would be perfect."

"Would the two of you prefer to share a bottle?"

Zane gave a small shake of his head. "I'd like a beer." He asked for one of the craft beers on tap.

"Would you care for an appetizer?" He glanced at Sarah, who shrugged. "Give us a few minutes to decide." When the waitress left, he caught Sarah's attention. "What do you think?"

"Of this place? It's fabulous. I can't believe all the work was done and I never heard anything about it. Do you know the name?"

He turned the menu to the front page. "The English Garden."

Her eyes sparked with amusement. "Of course." Opening the menu, her gaze ran over the offerings. "There's a lot to choose from. What are you ordering? Wait, let me guess. You're going for the ribeye steak."

"Orange roughy with quinoa."

"You're kidding."

Setting the menu aside, he shifted his chair in order to stretch out his long legs. "Nope. Being in the Army and working for a company in Southern California expanded my diet. What about you?"

"The glazed salmon with country salad. Fair warning, I'm saving room for dessert. They have fresh peach cobbler with homemade ice cream."

"You've sold me."

When the waitress delivered their drinks, Zane ordered the stuffed mushroom appetizers, and both gave her their dinner selections. Picking up his glass, he tipped it toward Sarah.

"To a great meal."

She touched her glass to his before taking a sip of the cold, white wine. "This is very good."

"Let's hope *everything* is good tonight."

Sarah hoped so, too.

Rona sat across from a man twenty-five years her senior, a family friend visiting Montana. He'd lost his wife to cancer a few months earlier, deciding a long vacation might help him get over her death.

Picking up her glass of wine, Rona took a sip while watching another table over the rim. Zane Talbot sat with a young woman with shoulder length, dark blonde hair. Her location provided a perfect view of their table on the wide porch.

She'd made inquiries about him after leaving the stables. Nobody had a bad word to say about the ranch hand. He was considered a hard worker, and a person who could be counted on when needed. No one mentioned a girlfriend, yet there he was, his complete attention on the woman next to him.

"Your father wasn't specific on your reasons for moving to Montana, Rona. I'll admit I'm baffled by your choice of locations." The man sipped his drink, relaxing back into his chair.

Gaze moving from Zane, she gave a small shrug. "I researched several areas in the western U.S., and visited a few. My preference was a place with changes of season."

"But why leave Texas at all?"

"It was time. Escaping the extreme heat also played a part in my decision." She stared into her wine glass, deciding to be honest. "Daddy isn't the easiest man to be around, but you already know this, George."

"You don't have to explain. He's hard and driven. It's what has made him successful. Unfortunately, his manner often drives away the people he cares about most."

Her attention moved to the window and the table outside. It had been a long time since she'd had any reaction to a man. Something about Zane fascinated her.

The girlfriend was a complication. Nothing Rona couldn't handle. She'd known plenty of men already in a relationship. Soon, the relationship they had was with her. She saw no reason the same couldn't happen with Zane.

Her thoughts were interrupted by the appearance of the waitress carrying their meals. They ate in silence for several minutes before Rona broke the silence.

"How long do you plan to stay in Whiskey Bend?"

Swallowing a bite of steak, George washed it down with water. "A month. Maybe longer. I have nothing that requires my attention back home."

"No current cases?"

"I've passed them along to other attorneys. They took care of my clients during Jerilyn's illness." He sat for a moment, the fork poised in the air. "I have an experienced and dedicated group of men and women. I've no doubt they'll do an exceptional job during my absence."

"There's a very competent law firm in town. Lawson and Chapman. I worked with Janet Chapman when purchasing my property. Her husband, Larry Lawson, is the senior partner."

Pushing the dinner plate away, he lifted the cup of coffee. "I'll stop by and introduce myself. Now, tell me what, or who, you're watching outside."

She chuckled at his awareness. "I should've known you'd catch me. The stable manager where I'm boarding my horses is at a table."

"There's more to it than that. You can hardly keep your eyes off him."

"It's nothing, George. He's attractive. Any woman would stare at him." When he cocked his head, she let out a sigh. "He's also here with someone, so it's hands-off."

A slow grin appeared, along with an amused glint in George's eyes. "I've known you since you were in kindergarten, Rona. I can't remember a time when you didn't go after something you wanted."

"Who says I want him? I'm curious is all. He's with a woman a little, well, less than I'd expect."

Turning in his seat, George spotted the couple, studying both people. Shifting back around, he gave her a contemplative look.

"She's quite pretty. My suggestion is you focus your attention on upgrading the property and getting to know the area. You don't need to start your life in Whiskey Bend by inserting yourself into an existing relationship. It's never worked out well for you, Rona."

She knew he was right. What George didn't know was the extenuating circumstances pushing her to learn more about Zane's relationship with the blonde.

"Don't worry. I'm not going to alienate anyone. Definitely not the stable manager." The lie came easily, as they all did.

Chapter Eight

Zane grasped Sarah's hand tighter as they walked to her front door. He wished the evening didn't have to end. The unexpected desire to stay with her a while longer engulfed him, undermining his firm resistance to a relationship.

Everything about the night had been better than expected. The food was excellent. The company even better. Sarah's wit and easy manner created an evening neither would forget. The question remained, what did he plan to do about it?

Reaching the door, Sarah shifted to look at him. "Would you like to come inside for a bit?"

He did, but wouldn't. "Yes, but I'd better head out. The Macklins, Kell, and I are meeting early to move the herd."

"Well, then, thank you for a wonderful time. Best night in I can't remember when." Rising on tiptoes, she brushed a kiss across his cheek. "Don't be a stranger, Zane."

"I don't intend to." Bending down, he wrapped an arm around her waist, tugging her against him. "Unless you object, I'm going to kiss you. And it won't be a brief brush across your cheek."

Meeting his intense gaze, she gave a slow nod. "All right."

The kiss was slow and penetrating, and all too brief. When he lifted his head, Zane realized whatever was happening between him and Sarah might be dangerous to his health. He studied her face before taking a step away.

"Do you have time to see me this week?"

"I'll make time, Zane."

"Good to know." Giving her a mock salute, he retraced his steps to the sidewalk.

Sliding into the driver's seat, he gripped the steering wheel with both hands. What was he doing? Sarah was Beth's cousin. Kell would kill him if things went south and he hurt her.

Starting the engine, he pulled onto the street, not looking to see if Sarah still stood on her porch. Debbie would've stayed until his taillights disappeared.

Is that what he'd been holding out for? A replacement for the fiancée he'd lost years earlier? The thought soured his stomach. Debbie could never be replaced. Not by anyone. It was the reason he'd never had a relationship since she died. He couldn't imagine another woman standing by his side, being his partner through the difficult challenges of life.

Believing this, why was he pursuing Sarah when he knew he could hurt her in the end? Zane didn't have an answer, other than he enjoyed her company.

Checking his rearview mirror, he spotted headlights coming up behind him. Not an issue, except their speed was well over the posted limit. The vehicle didn't slow as it came up to within a few feet of his rear bumper.

He didn't recognize the truck, and couldn't get a clear view of the driver or passenger. Zane didn't change his speed, pulling closer to the shoulder to give them plenty of room to pass. A mile sped by without the truck going around him.

Mental red flags dangled before him. It had been a year since he'd worked with Kell to provide information on their traitorous Army commander. Their participation in the investigation had almost cost them their lives. As remote as it seemed, he wondered if the passengers of the truck were out for vengeance. His grip on the steering wheel tightened.

Zane had made the decision to drive past the turn to Kell's house when the truck roared past him and kept going. A relieved breath blew from deep in his lungs. He didn't relax or immediately turn back toward Kell's.

Steering along country roads another fifteen minutes assured him the truck hadn't come back. The drive also gave him time to think a little more about Sarah and their budding relationship.

By the time he parked in the driveway, and against the warnings in his head, Zane had made up his mind to continue seeing her. Decision reached, he climbed out of the truck, his steps light as he entered the house.

Morning came too early for Sarah. She'd been awake most of the night, reliving dinner with Zane, and the much too short kiss.

She was no longer certain he wanted nothing except friendship. The kiss, though brief, held a heady heat Sarah would like to experience again.

Chastising herself for wasting time trying to find answers when none existed, she dragged herself out of bed. Dressing in her workout gear, she began to tick off her to-do list for the day.

Take a short run, followed by stretches and abs. Shower. Tackle her homework. Do the laundry. Head to the grocery store. Fix something simple for dinner. Slide under the covers, read, and hope for sleep.

Mentally going over the list again, she grimaced. Zane was right. Between work, school, and chores, she'd lost the spontaneity she used to embrace. Her life had become a monotonous replay of the same activities. Wash. Rinse. Repeat.

A self-deprecating grin spread across her face. She might be boring, but the thought didn't cause any regret over the decision to change her life. Thinking of the future excited and energized her. Nothing had ever felt so right.

Her phone chimed, playing Welcome Back, Kotter, the theme from a nineteen seventies sitcom about a teacher and his students. Checking the screen, she noted only a number appeared.

"Hello?"

"Hey, Sarah. This is Grace. Thorn's wife."

Wincing, she made a promise to put Grace's number in her contact list. "Good morning, Grace. How are you?"

"I'm fine. I wanted to let you know we're having a barbeque at the house this afternoon and would love it if you could join us."

Thinking of her long list for the day, she opened her mouth to decline. She thought of Zane. He would certainly be there.

"What time?"

"Come over about three. We'll eat around four."

"All right. What can I bring?"

"Hmmm. How about your brownies?"

"Great. Thanks for the invitation. I'll see you this afternoon." Hanging up, she rushed to make the brownies, thankful the ingredients were in the cupboard.

She placed the square baking pan into the oven, shut the door, and set the timer. Preparing the batter had kept her mind off Zane, if for just a few minutes. It had taken all her willpower not to ask if he'd be at Grace's.

The doorbell chimed, drawing her to the front door and away from thoughts of Zane. Taking a look through the peephole, she saw a tall, slender woman with a sleek brown bun at the back of her neck. She appeared to be wearing a windbreaker with a logo of a local running for public office.

Drawing the door open several inches, she forced a smile. "May I help you?"

"I'm working for candidate David Luong. He's running for city council. Do you know him?"

Sarah ran her gaze up and down the woman. Something about her seemed familiar. "Have we met?"

"Not to my knowledge." She checked her notes. "So, do you know Mr. Luong?"

"I've met him. He owns a mortgage company downtown."

Sarah continued to study the woman as she listed Luong's qualifications. She wondered how her appearance would change with her hair down, and without the large, round sunglasses. Sarah shifted to one side when the woman attempted to look into the house. After a few minutes of continued questions, the woman put her pen away.

"Thank you for your time. May I tell Mr. Luong you'll be supporting his candidacy?" Again, the woman tried to look past Sarah, who began closing the door.

"I haven't made up my mind. Have a nice day, Ms..."

Without answering, the woman turned away, rushing down the walkway.

"It was a little strange." Sarah placed the brownies on the counter while sharing the story of her visitor. "She didn't answer when I asked her name."

"What did she look like?" Grace set out a pasta salad, rummaging in a drawer for tongs.

"Taller than me by about three inches. Dark brown hair. She had it pulled into a bun, so I don't know how long it is, but at least to her shoulders."

"Heavyset or slender?"

"Slender. Her posture was excellent. Maybe she's an athlete." Sarah took the fork Grace held out, tasting a small amount of pasta.

Grace leaned a hip against the counter, crossing her arms. "Well, she could be one of at least a hundred women around Whiskey Bend. What made you uneasy about her?"

"It will sound silly, but she kept trying to look into the house. I tried to block her view, but her height would've provided a good view." She snagged a corn chip from a nearby bowl at the same time laughter came from outside.

"Sounds like the rest of the group is here." Grace left Sarah alone in the kitchen to greet her guests.

Lagging behind, she tried to stay busy adjusting the plates, utensils, condiments...anything to keep her thoughts from Zane. Heavy footfalls and loud voices signaled their entry into the house. She greeted the three Macklin brothers and their wives, plus Kell and Beth. There was no sign of Zane.

The disappointment was acute. Slumping a little, she told herself it would be best to put some time between them. A few days, maybe a week.

"Hello, Sarah."

She jumped at his voice coming from behind her, growing red with embarrassment. Several heartbeats passed before she felt the warmth of his hands on her waist, the brush of his lips across her neck.

"All right, you two, time to get to work." Grace breezed into the kitchen with Amy, Willow, and Beth following.

Sarah tried pulling away, but was held tight against Zane's chest. Seconds ticked by before he grabbed her hand, leading her into the living room to the women's laughter. Walking past the men, he led her out the back door.

She didn't attempt to tug her hand from his. "Where are we going?"

"I thought you'd like to see the newest foal."

"I'd love to." She squeezed his hand as they headed to the barn.

It wasn't difficult to find the stall holding the foal and mother. Letting go of Zane's hand, she looked through the bars.

"Oh, my. She's adorable."

Zane moved to stand beside her. "*She* is actually a *he*. A quarter horse colt."

"What's his name?"

"I don't believe he's been named. There's time to offer up your ideas."

Sarah laughed. "Me? I wouldn't have a clue what to name him. Is he registered?"

"He is. The owner can name him anything they want, though."

"Who's the owner?" Sarah assumed it was Thorn and Grace.

Watching the colt hide behind his mother, his eyes softened. "Me."

Chapter Nine

"Then Zane told me he was the owner." Sarah smiled at the elderly resident of the nursing home. "The colt is so cute."

The woman stared at her in rapt attention. "And this hunky man of yours said you can name him?"

"Well, he is hunky, but he's not really mine. We're just friends."

The woman waved a pale, bony hand patterned by numerous blue veins in the air. "Rubbish. If he took you to the English Garden, he's more than a friend." She wiggled a finger toward Sarah. "Or he wants to be more. You must pay attention, young lady. Signs are everywhere. All you have to do is watch for them."

Stifling a chuckle, Sarah helped the woman into a custom-made, upholstered chair by the window. "Here you go. May I get you a pillow, or your book?"

"Don't change the subject."

Tilting her head to the side, Sarah stilled with the woman's lap blanket in her hand. "What?"

"We were discussing your young man. Believe me. Any man who would let a woman name a horse holds serious interest in her. He wants more than friendship from you, Sarah."

An hour later, the words of the older, and wiser, woman still wafted through her. The idea of Zane having more than a cursory interest in her awakened the butterflies lodged in her stomach. She could feel them trilling, even as she took several deep breaths to calm them.

The barbeque had gone well. Zane had stayed by her side, breaking off to talk with the other men a few times. When she left, so did he, following her home, where they watched a movie. Afterward, he'd kissed her long and deep before heading home.

Sarah feared her emotions were getting too involved, overcoming her natural instinct to keep him at a distance. He chipped away her defenses each time they were together. Yesterday, at Thorn and Grace's, proved how easily he breached her emotional barricades.

And the man could kiss.

Flushing, she moved on to the last resident on her list. The man had been a resident of the home for several months. An unobtrusive patient, he kept to himself, preferring books to visitors. Today, he held a newspaper in his hands.

"How are you doing today, Mr. Weinbaum?"

Lowering the paper, he eyed her as if she intended to rob him. Then a miserly grin formed. "Good, good." He shook the paper. "Never anything good in this. I don't know why I bother." He tossed it toward his bed, missing by several inches.

Picking up the paper from the floor, Sarah folded it, setting it on the bedside table. "You could watch the news on your television." She adjusted the blinds, opening them for a better view of the garden.

"Rubbish. All of it."

"You do have a computer. There's lots of news you can read about."

Shaking his head, he pointed to the laptop his daughter had given him for his birthday. "Too much to remember. Usernames, passwords. And the print is too small to read."

Continuing to straighten up his room, she moved to the desk. "Would you like me to show you how to adjust the size of the font?"

"Fine, fine." Grabbing the nearby cane, he shoved up from the chair. "Show me something else I can forget."

By the time Sarah left the room, Mr. Weinbaum sat at the desk, his concentration focused on the computer screen. She was certain he'd have more to complain about when she came by tomorrow.

Finishing her rounds, she changed in the employee lounge, retrieved her purse from the locker, waved to the woman at the front desk, and stepped outside into a beautiful afternoon. Sarah had little time to grab an early dinner and make it to her class.

"What will it be tonight?" The murmured question was the same one uttered each time she made the transition from worker to student. "Chinese? Mexican? A sandwich?"

Making a turn toward the college, she pulled into the drive-through at the best Chinese restaurant in town. Checking her rearview mirror, her gaze landed on the driver of the car behind her. She sucked in a sharp breath, glancing away.

The woman could've been the twin of the door-to-door worker for city council candidate David Luong. Easing her car up, she looked again. There was no doubt the driver was the woman who'd come to her house.

Coincidence? She supposed it could be, though instincts warned her otherwise. Edging up to the window, Sarah paid, took her order, and pulled onto the street. Instead of stopping at the window, the car behind her pulled out of line to follow her.

Anger and fear mingled within Sarah. She slowed to see if the woman would go around her. The driver stayed ten feet behind her, close enough for Sarah to read a couple digits from the license plate, but not the full number. Picking up speed, she headed for the community college.

Reaching toward her purse, she fumbled inside for the phone. By the time she pulled it free, she'd turned into student parking and the first available space.

Quickly checking behind her, not spotting the woman or her car, she struggled with who to call. Sarah knew one person in law enforcement. Del Macklin.

Pulling up his number, her finger hovered over the call icon. What would she say? A woman followed me from Taco Dan's to the college, then disappeared. She remembered two digits of the license plate. Would that help?

Dropping the phone in her lap, she took several calming breaths. Sarah told herself the woman being at the Chinese restaurant was a coincidence and nothing more. Then why did she pull out of line without getting her food?

She didn't know what to do. Picking up the phone, she stared at it for several seconds before slipping it back into her purse. After her class, she'd call Beth and share what happened. If her cousin thought she should call Del, Sarah would.

Zane climbed from his truck, stretched, then stepped onto the sidewalk. He'd made plans to meet Thorn's business partners and good friends, Josh Reyes and Tony Coletti, at Wicked Waters. Both were single, and the same as Zane, had no plans to change their status.

Which was the reason he'd agreed to meet them for a beer. His growing affection for Sarah bothered him. Spending time with a woman whose company he enjoyed posed no threat. The problem came from his expanding feelings for the vivacious blonde with emerald green eyes.

"Hey, Zane." He glanced up to see Josh hold out a hand toward him. "Good to see you, man."

They shook hands, drawing each other into a bro hug. "It's been too long, Josh. How's everything?"

"Good. Busy." He opened the door. "We've got more work than we can handle at the shop." He nodded toward the semi-dark interior. "Tony's already inside."

Letting his eyes adjust, Zane took a quick look around. At seven, the place was already three-quarters full. About right for a Thursday night. There'd be no chairs or stools available in another hour.

"It's been too long, Zane." Tony slapped him on the back. "It appears ranch life agrees with you."

"Can't complain." Zane relaxed as the waitress set three beers on the table. Grabbing one, he tipped it toward Josh and Tony. "To us."

His gaze roamed the room again, a habit from his days as a Ranger. This time, he spotted the woman he'd danced with a few weeks earlier. The woman who inspired him to get out of the house and enjoy himself.

"Excuse me a minute, gentlemen." Picking up his beer, he sauntered over to where the woman stood with a couple friends.

Her eyes lit at the sight of him. "Hey. I remember you. Are you looking for a dance?"

"Why not?" Setting down his glass, Zane held out his hand. "I don't remember your name."

"Faith. Yours?"

"Nice to meet you, Faith. I'm Zane."

Leading her to the dance floor, they got in on the last minute of a two-step. The next was a slow dance. He took her into his arms, an unexpected sense of guilt consuming him. Was it because of Sarah?

"So, what do you do, Zane?"

"Work for some ranchers. We breed and train horses, and operate stables."

"Do you like it?"

"I grew up on a ranch near Bozeman. So, yes, I like it fine. What about you?"

"I teach at the community college. English and literature. Someday, I want to work for one of the major universities."

A teacher, the same as Sarah planned to be. As they danced, Zane couldn't help noticing how good Faith felt in his arms. Her height, at about five-feet-eight, fit his six-foot-two frame well. When the dance ended, he was tempted to keep her on the floor, deciding against it.

"Thanks for the dances, Faith. Maybe we can grab another before I leave."

"Anytime, Zane." Leaning up, she brushed a kiss across his lips.

Grabbing his beer, he headed back to the table. Josh and Tony watched him with curious expressions.

"I've danced with her before. Nice lady." More of an explanation than he'd planned.

Josh took a swallow of beer. "Thorn told us you were dating Sarah, Beth's cousin. That true?"

He thought a moment. Were they dating? Zane wasn't certain what they were doing, except he enjoyed her company. Then again, he enjoyed Faith's company, too.

"We've gone out for dinner. Does that constitute dating?"

"I guess Thorn thinks so," Tony said, glancing toward the dance floor.

"It's nothing serious. I'm not good relationship material."

Josh gave an emphatic nod. "I hear ya. Work keeps me too busy to try and fit in a woman."

"You don't want a family?" Zane asked.

"Haven't made up my mind. Nothing against marrying and having kids. It's just..." His voice trailed off when the woman Zane had danced with approached. She nodded at him before holding something out to Zane.

"I don't usually do this, but..." She handed him a piece of paper with her name and number. "Call me if you're ever in the mood to dance."

He stood, tucking the paper in his shirt pocket. Putting an arm around her waist, he drew her near, pressing a warm kiss over her mouth. The contact only lasted a couple seconds. Lifting his head, he patted his pocket.

"I'll do that, Faith." His gaze followed her as she left the saloon, wondering what he'd just done.

Josh took another swallow of beer. "Gorgeous woman. You gonna call her?"

Zane answered with a shrug.

Chapter Ten

Sarah dropped her purse and books on the table, too tired to do much except head to the bedroom. Undressing, she stepped into the shower, letting the warmth envelope her. Three hour classes always sapped her energy, and tonight's was more intense than most. She left with four pages of notes and two homework assignments.

"You can do this, Sarah." She murmured those words to herself often these days.

Rinsing shampoo from her hair, she washed her body, feeling the hot water relax her aching muscles. Drying off, her mind went to Zane, wondering what he was doing tonight.

It was Thursday, and she hadn't heard a word from him since Sunday at the barbeque. He'd mentioned calling, maybe doing something this weekend. She knew how busy they were with the stables and breeding program. He'd probably forgotten.

Disappointed, yet understanding his busy schedule, she slipped into sleeping pants and a lightweight sweatshirt. Drying her hair took several minutes, and the entire time, her thoughts were on Zane.

She'd promised herself not to let him draw her in, yet that's exactly what was happening. Her schedule was as bad as his, with no room for a relationship. Then why did she feel so disheartened?

"Enough of this, Sarah." Padding to the kitchen, she brewed a cup of chai tea, lowering herself onto the sofa when it was ready. Taking a sip, she stilled at a knock on her door.

Her first thought was of the woman who seemed to be popping up everywhere. When the knock came again, she set down the tea, turned on the outside light, and checked the peephole.

"Zane," she whispered before opening the door with an infectious smile "What are you—"

It was all she got out before he wrapped an arm around her waist, tugging her to him. His mouth covered hers, hungry, insistent, demanding. Coaxing her mouth open, his tongue swept inside, tasting as his desire rose.

Kicking the door closed, he swept her into his arms, lowering them both onto the sofa. She was still warm and relaxed from her shower, and even wearing a sweatshirt, her body molded against his. He took one more deep kiss before lifting his head, almost laughing at the languorous look on her face.

"I missed you, Sarah." At that moment, he realized how much.

She ran a finger down his cheek and along his jaw. "I missed you, too."

"Good." Kissing her again, he let his hand move over her back. "You smell wonderful."

"I just got out of the shower."

"Maybe someday we'll take one together."

She studied his serious expression, sensing something weighed on him. "Is everything all right?"

An hour ago, he was filled with uncertainty. No longer. "Everything is perfect, sweetheart." He held her for several minutes before shifting her from his lap and onto the sofa. "I should let you get some sleep."

"You're leaving?"

He studied her a moment before giving an abrupt nod. "We both know I should."

Standing, she walked him to the door, raising her face for a goodnight kiss. When both were breathing hard, they said their goodbyes, but not before he asked her to spend Sunday with him. Closing the door behind him, she couldn't stop her heart from pounding.

"Wow," she muttered, pressing a hand over her chest.

Zane took several deep, cleansing breaths on the way to his truck. He'd been uncertain about stopping by, not sure what to expect.

He'd left Wicked Waters in a state of confusion. There'd been no one in years, yet he now faced a possible choice between two wonderful women. Though Sarah already held a place in his life, Faith was a compelling woman. He knew she wouldn't turn him down if he called.

Without examining the reason, he drove to Sarah's. He hated uncertainty. Seeing Sarah, still damp from a shower, smelling of vanilla, lavender, and her own unique scent, he pushed thoughts of Faith from his mind.

He knew Sarah, understood her as a woman with little family support and a great deal of determination. She accepted everyone for what they were, without passing judgment. His best friend, Kell, married her cousin. A woman he respected and liked. All the Macklin wives loved her. He couldn't imagine anyone else fitting into his life with such ease.

Zane could see himself with Sarah for a solid stretch of time. Maybe not forever, but for as long as they got along.

Driving down the main street, he stopped at a light, spotting two women on the sidewalk. Recognizing Rona Kessler, he sighed. She'd moved her horses to the stables the day before. As he suspected, all four were magnificent animals.

What he hadn't expected was Rona's obvious interest in him. She'd found several opportunities to touch him, run a finger down his arm. When preparing to leave, he'd stepped away to avoid her kissing his cheek.

Rona was a gorgeous woman. Most men would find excuses to be with her instead of finding ways to avoid her. For some strange reason he couldn't identify, she irritated him. It wasn't her aggressive nature. He'd known other forceful women, even went out with one a few times. Regardless, the real reason for his edginess when near Rona, she was a client, which meant strictly off-limits.

When the second woman shifted, giving him a better view of her, his breath caught. He blinked several times, knowing his eyes and lack of light combined to deceive him.

The woman with Rona bore an uncanny resemblance to someone he used to know. The hair was a different color and much curlier. From a distance, her face appeared to be narrower, her curves more pronounced.

Rubbing his eyes, he shot one more look at the woman, assuring himself he'd never seen her before. There were tiny similarities and nothing more.

The driver behind Zane honked, forcing him to move on. He knew he'd never seen the woman before. Still, the resemblance shook him.

Forcing himself to relax, he rolled his neck at the next stop sign. He felt foolish. Whoever the woman was, he didn't know her. His mother told him everyone had a twin somewhere in the world. Tonight, he'd seen Debbie's.

"Do you have time to show another potential client around? If not, I can move an appointment."

Zane looked up from his desk to meet Kell's serious eyes. "What time?"

"After lunch. A woman who heard about us. She bought a house with a barn, corral, and pasture. No arena, round pen, and no direct access to riding trails."

Crossing his arms, he leaned against the doorjamb. "Let me guess. She just realized how much work it would be to keep horses at her place?"

Kell snickered. "Pretty much."

"How many horses?"

"Two. Both geldings. One is ten, the other twelve. Can you meet with her?"

"Sure. I have to be here anyway. Willow's sending a couple men out with the supplies we ordered."

"Does this include the supplements for Rona Kessler's horses?"

"They were on the order."

"Great. If the lady today signs a contract, we'll be full." Kell removed his hat, running a hand through his hair. "May have to move up finishing the second barn."

"And start the third one. I'd rather have too much space than not enough. I believe we'll get busier as we close in on winter."

"Might be the case. I'll talk to Boone, see where we're at with the bank loan." Settling his hat back on his head, Kell headed to the door. "I'm going to walk over there. Boone wants to talk about the breeding program."

"Should we all be there for that discussion?" Zane found he had a talent for breeding horses, and was pulled into most meetings.

"He wants to call a regular get-together this weekend. Maybe Sunday."

"I'm going to spend some time with Sarah on Sunday. Late afternoon would be great."

"I'll pass it by Boone. I heard you, uh...kissed a woman at Wicked Waters the other night."

Massaging the back of his neck, Zane shook his head. "I should've known Josh would share."

"Don't blame Josh. I heard it from Kull Kasey, who heard it from Tony Coletti." Hooking thumbs in the waistband of his Wranglers, Kell glared at Zane. "I won't take it well if you play around with Sarah while messing with another woman."

"You're right. I figured it out for myself the same night. Faith is a tempting woman, but Sarah is the one I want to get to know. No promises about where it will go, but I'm not planning to hurt her. I just hope Sarah doesn't hear about my brainless action at the saloon."

"The boys won't tell her. That's not to say one of her girlfriends wasn't there. Hell, she and Faith might know each other from the college." He clasped Zane on the shoulder. "I'd better get going. Watch for a woman of about twenty-eight. Can't miss her. She'll be the one driving a white Chevy dually." Kell chuckled as he headed out.

"Hey! What's her name?"

Kell just waved his hand in the air and kept walking.

The sound of a big engine drew Zane's attention away from a stack of paperwork. A jacked-up white Chevy truck bumped over the dirt drive, stopping in front of the office.

A sparkplug of a woman jumped down, adjusted her shirt and jeans, and looked around before marching toward the office.

He guessed her to be no more than five-feet-two, with broad shoulders, and short, spikey hair with purple tips. A woman who knew what she liked.

Opening the door, he held it open as he stuck out a hand. "Zane Talbot. Kell said to expect you."

Giving his hand a forceful pump, she smiled. "Jillian Pepper."

"Pleased to meet you, ma'am."

Dropping his hand, she waved it in the air. "Call me Jill or Jillian, but not ma'am. Makes me cringe. So, are you my tour guide?"

"My main talent."

Letting her gaze wander over him, she shook her head. "I doubt that. Well, I'm ready when you are."

By the time she drove out an hour later in her beast of a truck, they'd filled all the stalls in barn one. Jill would be bringing over her geldings on Saturday, along with tack and her own supplements.

He'd already agreed to show her the trails leading to the national park. It would be a short ride, maybe an hour. Zane considered inviting Sarah, warming to the idea the more he rolled it around in his head. Getting her out in the fresh air would help her relax, plus he'd bet a week's pay Sarah and Jill would get along great.

If only he'd known how right he was.

Chapter Eleven

"I'd love to go on the trail ride, Zane. What time should I be there?" Sarah had listened to his voice message while on break at the nursing home, excited he'd thought of her. Calling him back, she hadn't tried to hide her excitement.

"Nine. The new client will be here with her horses at seven-thirty. I'll have our horses tacked up by the time you get here."

"Perfect. Thanks for inviting me."

"I want to see you before tomorrow, Sarah. How about dinner at Doc's Grill?"

She ignored the warning bells telling her their relationship was moving too fast. "All right. What time should I meet you there?"

"Does seven work for you?"

"Works fine. I don't have class on Friday evenings, so any time after six is good."

"Great. I'll pick you up at six-thirty. See you then." He ended the call before she could repeat her suggestion to meet him.

She'd planned to walk the short distance between her house and the restaurant, giving herself some much needed quiet time. Considering her options, Sarah decided she'd love Zane's company.

Finishing the rest of her shift, she drove straight home, her mind filled with thoughts of him. Intriguing, smart, and handsome, he'd attracted the attention of many single women in Whiskey Bend. She'd heard the comments herself. At the grocery store, gas station, and when she'd met Beth at Wicked Waters.

Sarah found herself wondering why she was the woman who'd garnered Zane's interest. Perhaps for the same reason she found *him* so compelling. He fit into her world.

His best friend was Kell, her cousin's husband. He'd been welcomed as an honorary member of the Macklin family. Whether they were together or not, she'd be part of his life for as long as both stayed in Whiskey Bend.

Taking a quick shower, she dried her hair, her excitement at seeing Zane growing. Dinner tonight and a trail ride tomorrow. And unless he changed his mind, they would be spending Sunday together.

She pulled comfortable jeans from a drawer. They fit her figure without making her look as if they'd been painted on. Since the air outside would be cool, she slipped into a lightweight, long-sleeved silk top in pale peach. Checking the jewelry box on her dresser, Sarah retrieved a pair of gold earrings punctuated with semi-precious stones.

Sliding her feet into woven leather sandals, she grabbed her purse at the same time the doorbell chimed. Dormant butterflies in her stomach came to life.

Sarah closed the distance between her bedroom and front door in a few long steps. Not wanting to appear too eager, she stood for a moment, forcing herself to breathe in and out. Grabbing the knob, she drew it open.

"Hello, Sarah."

"Good evening, Zane. Would you like to come in, or do you want to leave now?"

"Doc is holding a table for us, so we should probably leave. Is walking all right?"

"Perfect."

Threading his fingers through hers, neither spoke for long seconds. Zane broke the silence.

"I'm glad you were available tonight."

"Me, too. I generally spend Friday evenings doing homework, but I was able to get most of it done during the week. Mainly because of your invitation to spend Sunday together."

Zane squeezed her hand, crossing the street toward downtown. "Sunday was too long before seeing you. Jill, the new client, decided to board her horses with us, and asked me to show her the trails. Adding you as a threesome was easy. You'd already mentioned riding, so..." He shrugged. "Dinner tonight is me wanting to spend more time with you."

"For two people not looking for a relationship, this is pushing things a little."

He came to an abrupt halt, shifting to look down at her. "Is this getting uncomfortable for you?"

"Not at all. Well, maybe a little. You didn't hear me hesitating when you called, did you?" She reached up, stroking a finger along his jaw.

Chuckling, he bent down to press a kiss against her lips before continuing toward the restaurant. "Not a hint of hesitation."

"Just an observation."

"We can slow it all down, Sarah. Saying no to an invitation won't upset me." He glanced back down at her turned up face. "Not much, anyway."

Laughing, she relaxed. Sarah enjoyed his easy humor. Falling in love with Zane Talbot would be much too easy, which worried her more than a little. She couldn't afford to lose sight of her goals for the company of a good-looking man. Not even Zane.

Opening the door to Doc's, he motioned her inside. Diego "Doc" Martinez stood at a table across the room, taking an order. Lifting his chin in recognition, he finished writing down the couple's selections before joining them at the hostess station.

"Good to see you, Zane. And you, too, Sarah. It's been a while."

"You know how it goes, man. Sarah's working and taking classes, and those Macklin brothers are slave drivers." Zane smiled, placing a hand on the small of her back.

"Well, you're here now, and I have the perfect table for you." Grabbing menus, Doc motioned for them to follow him across the room. "Hope this works for you."

The table sat in a small alcove with a window to the street, and clear view of the other tables. The best location in the place.

Doc took their drink orders. "I'll also bring bread and an appetizer while you review the menu. There are several new items."

"Thanks, Doc." Zane placed his hand over Sarah's. "Have you ever tried one of Doc's sample appetizers?"

"No. What will it be?"

"That's the beauty of it. You don't know until he brings it." Zane took a long swallow of water. "The sample appetizers aren't on the menu. He uses them to gauge how popular they'll be. I've never had one that wasn't incredible."

"Do most make it onto the menu?"

Nodding, Zane glanced around the room. A few people looked familiar. "He rotates them. Doc says he gets bored offering the same items every night. Appetizers are the easiest to change up."

"Here you are." Doc set down their drinks, then with a flourish, placed a small platter of appetizers on the table. "There are two kinds. Deep fried deviled eggs with maple bacon jam, and sriracha crème fraîche, smoked paprika, and garlic shrimp, with sourdough toast points."

Sarah inhaled the mingling aromas of the food. "These look wonderful, Doc."

"I'll want your honest feedback. Are you ready to order or should I stop back?"

"Do you know what you want, Sarah?"

Nodding, she pointed to the seafood section of the menu. "The grilled salmon with dill butter sauce."

"Excellent choice. And you, Zane?"

"The black and blue ribeye. Medium rare."

Doc snorted, giving a slight shake of his head. "One of these days, you should order something new."

Zane placed a hand over his heart. "I love your ribeye."

"Trust me. You'd love the elk tenderloin even more."

Searching it out on the menu, he read the description. "Fine. I'll give it a try."

"Once you taste it, you might never go back to the ribeye." Doc made another note before returning to the kitchen.

"He hasn't moved to electronic orders?" Sarah took a sip of her wine, relaxing against the back of her chair.

"Says it's too hard to add special requests. Personally, I believe he simply prefers a pad and pencil." Taking a deep swallow of his draft beer, Zane leaned forward.

"How were classes this week?"

"The same as most classes. Challenging. Some of the information even interesting." Grinning, she took another sip of wine before setting down the glass to select an appetizer. Tapping a finger against her lips, she studied the two deviled eggs, then moved her attention to the shrimp. "Which one first? I think an egg."

Picking up the platter, Zane held it out to her. "Take whatever you want."

She took one of each, waiting to try them until Zane had taken his own. Deciding to try the deviled egg first, she cut a small bite.

"Oh, my gosh. This is fantastic. If you don't want yours, I'll take it." She was only partially joking.

"Not a chance, gorgeous." He scooped up the egg, slipping it into his mouth. His eyes sparked, a slight smile appearing on his face as the flavors melded together. "You're right. This is amazing."

"Ready to try the shrimp?" Sarah asked.

Washing the last of the egg down with his beer, he waited for her to place a shrimp in her mouth. She chewed slowly, closing her eyes to focus on the flavors.

"Well?"

Setting down her fork, she rested her chin in a hand. "It's horrible, Zane."

"Right." He ate his own, nodding in appreciation. "Both of these should be on the menu."

"I'm glad you brought me here. Beth and I have come together, but Doc never offered us samples."

"Might be because he only creates them on Fridays and Saturdays." He reached out a hand, covering hers as Doc appeared with their entrees.

"Salmon for the lady, and elk tenderloin for the gentleman. Can I get you anything else?"

Sarah shook her head.

"I think we're good for now," Zane answered. "The appetizers were both great. Are you getting the same feedback from everyone else?"

"Pretty much. Both will be rotated into the menu starting next weekend. I'll leave you to your meals."

They made small talk while enjoying their dinners. Zane couldn't praise his steak enough, wondering how he'd never tried it before.

"You're a creature of habit, Zane. I'll bet you've never read the entire menu." She slid another bite of salmon into her mouth.

"You'd be right. Guess I should start."

"Hey, aren't you Zane? You're friends with Josh and Tony."

He hadn't seen anyone approach. Setting down his fork and knife, he stood, holding out his hand. "Zane Talbot."

They shook before the man chuckled. "Bob Carson. My buddy and I were in Wicked Waters the other night. You and that stunning woman you were dancing with provided the best entertainment of the night."

Zane's stomach tanked. He'd never thought his actions would get back to Sarah. Risking a glance at her, he winced at her bewildered expression.

"Faith is one gorgeous female. And that kiss." The man clasped him on the shoulder. "Well, I'll let you get back to your meals. Have a great night."

Lowering himself into his chair, Zane tried to take hold of her hand. She was faster, moving it out of his reach.

"Who's Faith?"

"It isn't what you think."

Touching her napkin to the corners of her mouth, she set it on the table. "I'm not sure what I think. Why don't you explain it to me?"

Chapter Twelve

Sarah knew they were hovering on territory never discussed. Neither had mentioned being exclusive, and to be honest, all they'd ever shared were meals and a few kisses.

"You know what? Never mind. What you do with your free time is none of my business."

Ice formed in his stomach as his mind raced. How did he explain something that sounded bad on the surface? Ignoring her comment of his personal life being none of her business, Zane made an effort to explain.

"Faith is a woman I've danced with a couple times at Wicked Waters. Dances, Sarah, and nothing more. I don't even know her last name. Before she left the other night, Faith handed me a piece of paper with her phone number. The kiss was a stupid move, which meant nothing."

Sarah gave a slow nod, not responding.

"I wouldn't be here with you if there was anyone else." Picking up his beer, he emptied the bottle, setting it down a little harder than necessary. He needed to get his irritation under control.

Holding up both hands, she offered a too bright smile. "You don't have to explain. We're both adults and can see whoever we want." Lowering her hands, she clasped them in her lap.

"So we're clear, I am not seeing anyone but you, Sarah."

"All right." Her gaze flashed on her empty plate. "Do we have time for dessert?"

Zane chuckled, thankful for her acceptance of an awkward situation, and her sense of humor. "Sure. In fact, I believe it's required." Snagging the dessert menu from the empty table next to them, he handed it to her.

Scanning it, she met his expectant gaze. "There are no bad choices. What do you suggest?" She handed him the menu.

"I've only had the chocolate lava cake with ice cream. Kell likes the Tiramisu. Get two if you can't decide."

Her laugh this time held a little more humor. "Berry cobbler with ice cream."

Getting Doc's attention, Zane ordered her cobbler, and lava cake for himself, plus two coffees. Setting the menu down, he leaned back, crossing his arms. He couldn't come up with anything to say, and was thankful the desserts didn't take long to arrive.

The walk back to Sarah's house held a slight chill. Halfway there, he laced his fingers with hers, glad she didn't pull away.

He knew she was right about their personal time being private. They weren't in an exclusive relationship. Not even a week ago, he would've laughed at the thought. Now, he wasn't so sure. The idea of hurting her bothered him.

"I'm not seeing anyone else, either." Her voice was so low he almost missed it.

He squeezed her hand. "I didn't think you were."

Stepping onto her porch, both hesitated. "Am I still invited on the trail ride?"

Wrapping an arm around her waist, he tugged her to him. "I'd be very disappointed if you didn't show up. Same with Sunday."

"Good, because I'm looking forward to both. What time on Sunday?"

"I'll pick you up about eleven. I thought we'd drive into Missoula, have lunch. Not sure what else. I just want to spend time with you."

She graced him with a cautious smile. "Sounds good."

Studying her features, he didn't see the eagerness she showed before dinner. Zane knew his antics with Faith were the reason for the change. He couldn't undo the damage a simple act created.

Instead of kissing her, he brushed his lips across her forehead. "I'm looking forward to the trail ride tomorrow."

"So am I."

Watching him pull away from the curb, Sarah tried to summon more enthusiasm for the weekend. The kiss wasn't such a big issue. Not for Sarah.

Her sympathies rested with the woman she'd never met. Did Faith believe Zane had feelings for her? Was she expecting a call? Had he humiliated her, or was his kiss welcomed?

Checking the time, Sarah grabbed her phone. It wasn't too late to call Beth. Maybe she'd heard of Zane's actions at the saloon. Perhaps she knew Faith. It wasn't unreasonable. Beth had been in Whiskey Bend a while, knew a great many people.

Finger hovering over Beth's number, she stared at the phone and sighed. She wouldn't bother her cousin with something so trivial. As she'd told Zane, their relationship wasn't exclusive. Then why did it feel as if it was?

Neither were dating anyone else. She'd never be able to fit more than one man in her crazy schedule.

As for Zane, he didn't seem to have the interest. Sarah wasn't a fool. He could change his mind at any time. Faith might be someone for his future, when he'd grown bored with her. Sarah's throat grew tight at the thought, a sure sign her feelings for him were moving in the wrong direction. Instead of keeping him at a distance, she found herself drawing closer each time they were together.

Sarah felt waves of exhaustion assault her. Retreating to her bedroom, she chided herself for spending so much time trying to evaluate a relationship that didn't exist. Work and school deserved all her attention.

Sitting on the edge of the bed, she closed her eyes, raising her head toward the ceiling. Work and school. Was there truly no time for anything else?

A smart woman would start backing away, make this weekend their last. Yawning, Sarah fell back on the bed, never opening her eyes. Doing what she should had always been more difficult than doing what she wanted.

Sarah knew it was a real dilemma, one which wouldn't be solved tonight.

Zane's fingers flew over his keyboard, code changing at light speed on his almost finished application for equine and bovine breeders. He didn't check the time, wouldn't care what the clock said.

The application had been his nighttime project for months. He'd spent hours in his bedroom in Kell's house testing, modifying, and testing again. Working on the application forced his mind away from everyday issues, requiring him to concentrate without distraction.

Unfortunately, his mind continued wandering to other matters. Sarah, Faith, the new boarders at the stables, the ranch breeding program, the woman who reminded him a little bit of Debbie.

Just two of those topics were important. Increasing the number of boarders and the breeding program. The other bullet points didn't matter. Not even the emergence of Sarah in his life.

His fingers stilled as an image of Sarah flashed in his mind. How had he let her become so important in such a short period of time? Zane didn't have an answer.

Forcing his attention back to the screen, he continued working. The program he'd designed would make it easier for ranchers to manage their boarding and breeding activities. An added benefit was the ease of use. Beta testing indicated training had been cut from weeks to a few days.

The work he performed now was in response to suggestions his beta testers gave him. It required complete focus, yet he couldn't seem to get Sarah out of his head.

Scrubbing his face with both hands, he exhaled a deep sigh. He'd done as much as his mind would allow tonight. Closing the computer, he stalked to the bed, rolling onto his back.

Checking the clock for the first time since he began fiddling with the app's code, he wasn't surprised to see four o'clock stare back at him. He had to be up in two hours to help their part-time ranch hand feed the horses, muck out the stalls, and lay bedding.

They'd have twenty horses when Jill arrived with her two geldings. A full barn, and four people on the waiting list for the completion of the second barn. They were off to a great start.

Resting an arm over his eyes, he closed his eyes, calming his mind. He'd done it plenty of times as an Army Ranger, but that had been a while ago. Short catnaps had been a part of his life. Not so much since leaving the service.

It felt as if seconds had passed when his eyes opened at the pinging of the alarm. Straight up six o'clock.

Shredding fingers through his hair, he slipped into Wranglers, a clean t-shirt, and plaid shirt. Taking a few minutes in the bathroom, he headed downstairs to the kitchen, following the aroma of fresh brewed coffee. Kell and Beth sat at the table, sipping from cups.

"I was just going to make breakfast," Beth said. "Eggs, bacon, and toast sound all right to you, Zane?"

"Great. Thanks." He poured a cup of coffee and checked out the window, seeing another clear, summer day emerge.

"Rico is already here, and he brought a friend who grew up on a ranch in Wyoming." Kell stood, walking to the counter to top off his coffee. "Rico will make sure Jill's stalls are ready before cleaning the rest of the barn. What time do you expect her?"

"Seven-thirty to eight. Sarah will be here closer to nine. The three of us will do a short trail ride so I can point out the trail into the national forest." Zane blew across his coffee before taking a sip. "We won't be gone more than an hour."

Kell joined him at the window. "I got a call late last night from Rona Keller. She asked if you could do the same for her."

Zane's brows drew together. "What?"

"Show her the trailhead. I told her it was easy to identify on the map, and the signs were clear. She insisted you show her personally."

"Not a chance, Kell. The lady's relentless."

"Relentless about what?" Beth held up a spatula, her other hand holding the handle of the fry pan.

Flashing a smile, Kell chuckled. "Seems Ms. Kessler has shown an interest in Zane."

"Really? How exciting." She plated eggs, toast, and bacon, holding it out to Zane.

"There's nothing exciting about unwanted attention." Setting the plate on the table, Zane let out a low growl. "I've done my duty by her. Find someone else to be her tour guide. Rico might be perfect." Digging into his breakfast, he didn't see the knowing look Kell sent Beth.

Taking a filled plate, Kell sat down next to Zane. "Rico would be happy to show her around."

Grunting in response, he didn't look up from his meal.

"You're getting quite the following, Zane." Beth set down her plate before pulling up a chair. "Sarah, Faith, and now Rona. Anyone I missed?"

This got his attention. Glancing up, his mouth twisted into a scowl. "Funny."

"It kind of is when you think about it." She scooped up a spoonful of eggs, slipping them into her mouth.

Shoving away his empty plate, Zane leaned back, crossing his arms. "How's that?"

"All this time and you haven't had anything to do with a woman. Now you have three vying for your attention."

"I wouldn't put it that way."

Beth picked up a glass of orange juice, finishing the contents. "Of course you wouldn't. By the way, how is Sarah?"

"She'll be here at nine. You can ask her yourself." Standing, Zane picked up his plate and cup, rinsing them in the sink before placing them in the dishwasher.

"I might do that."

Crossing his arms, Zane leaned against the counter. "You're welcome to come with us on the trail ride. It'll give you a chance to meet Jill, one of the new boarders."

"I might do that, too."

"We leave at nine. Let me know if you'll be joining us and I'll have Rico tack up your horse. I'm going to check out the stalls."

Kell listened to the exchange while sipping his now tepid coffee. Ever since Zane first showed an interest in Sarah, he'd been trying to figure out what triggered the change. Maybe Zane finally decided he'd grieved over Debbie long enough. Or perhaps his friend held a real interest in Sarah. Could be a combination of both. Whatever the reason, Kell was glad to see Zane break out of his decade long mourning for his dead fiancée.

As far as his new popularity, Kell looked forward to sitting back and enjoying the show.

Chapter Thirteen

"Jill, this is Sarah Hutchison and Beth Brooks. You've met Beth's husband, Kell. Ladies, this is our newest client, Jill Pepper." Zane walked to the rail where the four horses waited. "Anyone need help mounting?"

"Not me," Jill responded, mounting one of her geldings.

Shaking their heads, Beth and Sarah swung into their saddles. When all the ladies were ready, Zane mounted his own horse, reining it around to face them.

"This will be a short ride. We'll be going to the trailhead which leads into the national forest. That will take about thirty minutes. From there, we'll ride on about fifteen more minutes to where the main trail splits off into three. Those trails and most additional trails are on the map. That's where we'll turn around and head back. There are bottles of water and protein bars in your saddlebags. Everyone ready?"

"Ready, Zane." Jill edged up behind him, leaving Beth and Sarah to take up the rear.

They rode through three gates before heading into unfenced acreage. Zane called out landmarks but didn't narrate, though he looked behind him every few minutes to be certain the women were still with him. Not that they would disappear.

Reaching the trailhead, he reined up. Shifting his gaze to Sarah, he was aware they'd spoken less than a dozen words since she arrived. Even now, she didn't make a move to ride up to him. He hoped she'd stay for a while after they returned to the barn.

"If you look to the north, you'll see a parking lot between the trees. Most people trailer their horses to that spot and hit the trailhead from there."

"Convenience was a big reason I chose your stable, Zane." Jill nodded toward the parking lot. "I didn't want to trailer my horse for every ride. I'll also be able to ride alone if there's no one interested in going with me."

"I wouldn't recommend riding alone, Jill. At least not any farther than where the trail splits off. There are bears, cougars, and other predators in these mountains. Always carry your cell phone on your belt or in a pocket, not attached to the saddlehorn. You should also have bear spray in your saddlebag, along with whatever weapon you're comfortable using."

The women looked at each other, but didn't comment.

"Make sure you have water, protein bars, and rain gear. The weather changes quickly around here. I'm sure you all know this stuff, but I'd rather include it than assume. Let's ride to where this trail splits, then we'll head back."

Sarah rode past Jill to join Zane at the front. "Do you mind if I ride up here with you?"

"Not at all. The trail will narrow up here, then widens again. How are you doing?"

"Good. Sorry about last night. I shouldn't have pushed about Faith. It was just a kiss, right?"

His brows lowered. "Nothing more, Sarah. If you're up for it, I want to push the incident behind us and start over. What do you say?"

"I'd say that's an excellent idea." She grasped his outstretched hand for a moment before both returned their attention to the trail.

Zane and Sarah rode together until the group returned to the stables. Reining up outside the barn, his gaze moved to a small SUV parked close to where the second barn was under construction. He didn't recognize the vehicle or the driver, whose head was turned away from him.

A low groan slipped from his lips when Rona Kessler exited from the passenger side. He glanced away, hoping she hadn't spotted him. Reminding himself she could be at the ranch for a variety of reasons, he handed his reins to Rico, instructing him to groom his horse, as well as Sarah's and Beth's.

"Jill. Would you like Rico to cool your horse down?"

"Never used anyone before, and don't intend to start now. Thanks for pointing out the trails, Zane."

"Anytime, Jill." He joined Sarah at the back door of the house, taking another look at the SUV.

Rona was nowhere in sight, but he did get a better view of the driver's profile. Straight nose, rounded chin, full lips. Her hair was wavy brown, falling to just below her shoulders. He was certain it was the same woman he saw with Rona downtown. This time, there was no doubt she wasn't familiar. Then her face turned toward him.

Zane felt as if a mule had kicked him in the stomach. He told himself it was the eyes. They were the same almond shaped, startling blue he used to look into every day. Until she'd died in a car crash.

He told himself it wasn't her. Couldn't be the woman he'd planned to marry. Nothing else about her reminded him of the only woman he'd ever loved.

But the eyes. They drew him in, the same as ten years ago. He moved without thought toward the car, his gaze locked with hers. Before he covered the distance between them, a man appeared to his right, his hurried steps taking him to the driver's side. The woman, who looked so much like the love he'd lost it made his heart ache, rolled down her window.

The man bent down, said something, which caused her to start the engine. Seconds later, she drove off, never taking care not to glance back at him.

"Hey, man. You all right?"

Feeling as if he'd been gutted, Zane tore his attention away from the retreating car to look at Kell. He opened, then closed his mouth. Telling his best friend he may have seen a ghost wouldn't go over well. Besides, Zane didn't believe it himself. There had to be a hundred women with strikingly blue, almond shaped eyes.

"I'm fine. Do me a favor. Keep Rona away from me for a while."

Kell studied him a moment before crossing his arms on a laugh. "No worries. I'll make sure she doesn't get near you. She's not dressed for riding, so my guess is this will be a short visit."

Clasping him on the back, Zane let out a breath. "Thanks. I owe you."

"As if. Go on and get out of here. I've got enough help. Maybe you could take Sarah to the lake."

Scratching the back of his head, he nodded. "The lake is a great idea."

"Grab the fishing poles and tackle box from the garage. I heard the trout are thick at the south end." Kell didn't wait for a response before jogging away to intercept an approaching Rona.

They took Zane's truck to the lake. Sarah hadn't hesitated when he asked her to accompany him, even borrowing tennis shoes and lightweight pants from Beth. Lunch of sandwiches, fruit, and fresh baked cookies had been packed into a wicker basket, cold water and a couple beers in a cooler.

Per their agreement, this was an attempt at starting over. Both ignored the fact they'd barely started the first time. Zane didn't care, as long as his kiss with Faith was forgotten.

Grabbing everything from the back seat, they made their way down a narrow walking trail to the shore.

Primitive with few amenities, rocks and fallen logs were used for tables and chairs.

"Do you want to eat now or wait?" He set down the cooler, folding chairs, and fishing rods.

"Now. Then we can concentrate on catching trout." She placed the picnic basket next to the cooler.

A grin tipped a corner of his mouth. "A woman who isn't shy about wanting to eat."

"I've never seen a reason to hide the fact I'm hungry." Her stomach grumbled, as if emphasizing her point. "There you go." She laughed, opening the picnic basket. "Four sandwiches. Two turkey and two ham. I can only eat one."

Handing her a bottle of water, Zane glanced around. His senses were dancing, warning him they might not be alone. A scan of the area showed they were alone. He didn't believe it. Nor did he look at the food.

"Take whichever one you want and I'll eat the others." Walking to the edge of the water, he held up a pair of binoculars, taking his time scanning the lake and shoreline. He saw nothing to alarm him.

"What's wrong?"

Lowering the binoculars, he turned to face her. "Wrong?"

"Don't deny you're worried about something, Zane. I can tell by the way you're not jumping on the food."

Walking toward her, he chuckled. "I can control my desires." Wrapping an arm around her waist, he covered her mouth with his. A moment later, he raised his head. "Well, except when they involve you."

"Glad to hear it." She kissed him once more before stepping away. "Are you sure everything else is all right?"

"Fine. Just checking to see who we may be competing against for trout."

"And?"

"No one's out except us." He set the binoculars on a rock, picking up a sandwich and unwrapping it.

Sarah found a place to sit on a nearby log, taking a small bite of her sandwich. Zane took a seat next to her, proceeding to devour his sandwich in three bites. Draining a bottle of water, he leaned forward, resting his arms on his thighs.

Finishing her sandwich, Sarah held a fishing pole in the air. "Time to catch some trout, Talbot."

They selected spots ten feet away from each other. It didn't take long for Zane to realize Sarah was an experienced angler.

"Who taught you how to fish?"

Sarah shot a look at her string of four fish, then glanced at his one trout. "My uncle. He worked construction six days a week. On Sundays, after church, he'd take me fishing. He knew all the best spots, what bait to use, and the right lures. We were a great team."

"What happened to him?"

Her shoulders slumped for an instant before she looked at him. "He died. An on the job accident when I was thirteen. This is the first time I've fished since his death. Guess I haven't lost my touch." The smile she offered wasn't filled with joy.

"He must have been a great teacher. I've fished a lot, and never walked away with just one fish."

"We can keep going. I could fish all day." To prove it, she cast her line out into the lake.

Sitting down, Zane leaned back on his elbows to watch her. She was a sight with her dark blonde hair flowing around her shoulders. Every once in a while, she'd flash him a smile, which went straight to his heart.

He turned his head away, unable to accept his feelings for Beth's spunky cousin were deepening. This wasn't the way he'd planned it. He hadn't wanted anything permanent, yet this had the feel of long-term.

Letting his gaze wander along the shoreline, it came to a stop on a man he hadn't noticed before. He looked oddly familiar, and out of place in his khaki slacks and light yellow polo shirt.

What caught Zane's attention were the binoculars in the man's hand. Was he watching them?

Unease raced through him. Why would anyone have an interest in either Sarah or him? Pulling out his phone, he turned to take a picture of the man. He'd disappeared.

Maybe he was wrong. The man could've been a tourist, checking out the lake for a fishing trip. Or, like him and Sarah, getting out of the house for the day. Neither felt right to Zane.

Standing, he began packing up their gear. "Sarah, how about we head back to the ranch?"

Her brows lowered, but she nodded, reeling in her fishing line. "Sure."

"I have some stuff that needs my attention before tomorrow."

"No problem, Zane. I had a great time on the ride this morning, and fishing."

His heart thudded at her broad, genuine smile. "So did I."

Chapter Fourteen

"For the last time, Rona, I'm not going back out to the stables with you. Driving you out there this morning was a onetime thing. I have my own job, and you have your own car, plus a truck, and an SUV you can use. And don't try to make me feel guilty. It won't work."

"I don't understand why you're so against going out there, Tam. There are four horses which need riding. It would be fun to ride together. You should've stayed this morning instead of driving away."

Stirring the pot on the stove, Tamara O'Dell's lips stretched into a thin line. Rona could drive anyone nuts with her constant questions. This time, she wasn't going to give her the satisfaction of answers. Tamara's reasons for avoiding the ranch owned by Kell and Beth Brooks were private.

"I came back for you, didn't I?"

Pulling out a chair at a small table in the rustic kitchen, Rona sat down, cradling a cup of coffee. "You did. It would've been so much more fun if you'd stayed."

Using a spoon to dip out a small taste of stew, Tamara offered it to Rona. "Taste this. It's missing something."

Blowing on the spoon, Rona swallowed the sample. "It doesn't need much. Perhaps a little more marjoram. And a pinch of thyme."

Stirring in the two herbs, Tamara took another taste for herself. "Perfect."

"Tell me about your new job."

"Not much to tell. I'm working in the only feed store in Whiskey Bend. The pay and hours are good. The owner is Willow Macklin. She's married to the youngest Macklin boy, the one who runs the ranch."

"My understanding is they own part of the boarding stables." Standing up, Rona refilled her coffee cup. "Which reminds me. You have to meet the stable manager."

Tamara grabbed a couple bowls from the cupboard, filling each with stew. "Oh?"

"Definitely. I'd love to get his attention, but he's seeing Beth Brooks's cousin. Sarah something. The rumors around town are that he doesn't do relationships. So when he and Sarah split, I want to be right there, the first in line." She took the bowl Tamara handed her and sat down. "His name is Zane Talbot. Have you heard of him?"

"Um...no. Never heard of him."

Rona moaned on a spoonful of stew. "This is perfect, Tam. I'd love the recipe." She took another bite before putting the spoon down. "You must meet Zane and give me your opinion."

"If you like him, I'm sure he's amazing."

"He is. That's why I want you to go to the stables with me sometime. Not just drop me off, but stay for a while."

Finishing her stew, Tamara pushed her bowl away. "I don't understand."

"I want to know what you think of him."

Standing, Tamara picked up her bowl, shaking her head. "Whether I like him or not isn't important. We both know your family isn't going to let it go very far. As soon as they find out you're seeing him, they'll drag you back to Texas."

Snorting a laugh, Rona joined Tamara at the sink. "I'm well over eighteen. My parents can't drag me anywhere."

Incredulous, she crossed her arms, letting out a derisive snort. "They pay for everything you do. The horses are theirs. The property, house, and barn are in their names, not yours. You're given money each month to live on. Do you understand what I'm saying, Rona?"

"I have money from my grandmother."

"Which you can't touch until you're thirty. Even then, the payments come in increments over five years. Why don't you meet a handsome cowboy with money? Someone your parents will accept. No matter how many wonderful qualities, uh...what's his name?"

"Zane."

"Right. No matter Zane's qualities, unless he comes from wealth, you're out of luck. Plus, there's the issue of him already seeing someone. Do you truly want to bust that up for a short fling?"

"You've always been such a prude, Tam. If Zane really likes the girl, he won't let anyone come between them. If he doesn't..." Rona let the unfinished question hang between them.

Scooping out the remainder of the stew into a plastic container, she sealed the top, placing it in the refrigerator. "As always, you'll do what you want, but you're not dragging me into it. I'm not interested in going to the stables, and am less interested in messing up someone's life so you can enjoy a few good times. I'm going upstairs. There are bills to pay, then I'm taking a shower. You're welcome to crash here tonight."

"It's Saturday, Tam. Let's go to Wicked Waters and have some fun."

Leaning against the doorframe, she crossed her arms. "It's been a long week, and I'm exhausted. Maybe next Saturday we can go."

"Yeah, maybe. Do you mind if I clean up a bit and borrow some clothes? No sense driving back to my place, then coming all the way back to town."

"Sure. I've got plenty of jeans and shirts. I'll set some stuff out for you. Have a good time."

Heading down the hall, Tamara glanced around at the small, two bedroom house she rented. It had one full bath, and a half-bath with sink and toilet. Perfect for one person. She'd made up her mind the moment the realtor let her inside.

The yard was large enough for a small garden. It came with a barbeque, and table with four chairs. There were a few potted plants that needed extra care, and a big shade tree near the back fence. A swing had been secured to a large branch.

The front was just as quaint, with a porch, three Adirondack chairs, two tables, and several hanging plants. The owners had relocated to a small town north of Missoula after deciding Whiskey Bend was getting too large. She wasn't intending to sign a lease, but after seeing the house, decided to commit for one year.

Stepping into the shower, she washed her hair, letting the hot water sluice over her head and down her back. Another reason she'd rented the house. The water heater held seventy-five gallons. Washing her tired body, Tamara turned off the water, grabbing one of the thick towels she'd purchased.

Wrapping it around her, she sat on the edge of the bed and thought of the stables. Rona had talked of it often since signing the agreement for her four horses. She'd also spoken of Zane Talbot, though not as much as tonight.

Rona had been brought up on a huge Texas ranch, wanting for nothing. In contrast, Tamara's family had lived in a moderate sized home close to Dallas. Her father worked for a large construction company as a supervisor, while her mother was an administrative assistant for one of the company's executives.

Their fathers had been best friends since first grade. The families didn't get together often, yet somehow, Rona and Tamara remained friends.

Everything changed when Tamara turned fourteen. Both parents lost their jobs, forcing the family to sell their home and move out of Texas. They relocated several times over the years.

At twenty-five, her parents were killed in a multi-car pileup on the interstate. She'd been left with a house near Billings, Montana, and two life insurance policies. Tamara had rented out the house, placed most of the money from the policies in savings, and relocated to Helena, then Missoula, finally settling in Whiskey Bend when Rona decided to move out of Texas.

Unlike her friend, Tamara held no interest in dating or a relationship. Her job at Robinson's Feed and Tack, and part-time classes at the local community college, took all her time. She loved her work, which surprised her. When applying for the clerk position, Tamara saw it as a short-term job until finding more suitable employment. It hadn't been quite a month, yet she had no desire to apply for other work.

Removing the towel wrapped around her hair, she finger combed her wavy tresses as she thought about how her life had changed from the dreams she once held. She'd planned to marry, and maybe have at least one child by now.

Tamara's goals had shifted from love and family to short-term jobs, which supported her travels. Not that the list of places she'd visited had been extensive. She didn't even have a passport. Her immediate plans included traveling around the western United States. Maybe this year, she'd add Canada.

Rain slapped against his bedroom windows, disturbing Zane's concentration. He had too many loose ends in his life. One would be wrapped up by morning, assuming he made the corrections to the code over the coming hours.

There were other projects dancing around in his head, each waiting for him to carve out an appropriate amount of time. The big question was which one would be next?

Four companies showed an interest in his current project. Two venture capitalist firms, one third-party application company in the horse breeding and boarding space, and a foreign company anxious to break into the U.S. market. The fifth option was for Zane to negotiate his own licensing deal with an existing company supplying products for breeding and boarding customers.

Each would require weeks of due diligence. A small price to pay for the financial outcome he anticipated. The royalties would allow him to buy a place of his own, and plan for the future.

Tapping the keyboard at a furious pace, he worked for two more hours before sitting back to stare at the screen. He and the new application were ready for presentation to the interested parties.

Padding downstairs, he grabbed a bottle of water, emptying it in a few gulps. He thought of Sarah and their time at the lake. They'd had a great time until he'd spotted the man with the binoculars.

Zane chastised himself for not getting a photo of the stranger. His best estimate put the man in his forties to early fifties. About five-feet-eight, he had short hair, a ruddy complexion, and the look of someone working for the government. He'd known enough of them over the years to make him wary.

What he couldn't figure out was why an agent from any of the numerous government agencies would be in Whiskey Bend. The flip side was Zane was wrong in his assessment. He could be nothing more than a tourist curious about the lake.

Except for one thing. Zane was certain the man he'd seen walking up to the car Rona exited at the ranch and the man at the lake were the same. He'd spoken briefly with the other woman before she drove away.

Tossing the plastic bottle in a recycle bin, he returned to his bedroom, determined to sleep. His mind refused to cooperate. It wouldn't stop cycling between the computer application, the man at the lake, the woman driving the car, and his growing attraction to Sarah.

Of the four, the only one which brought him peace, leading him to sleep, was Sarah.

Chapter Fifteen

Sarah finished the last bite of her ground elk burger, popping one more delicious garlic fry into her mouth. Shoving the plate away, she sucked the last of her soda through a straw.

"How about dessert?" The young, very slim waitress stopped next to her, nodding toward the empty plate. "We have a great double chocolate brownie with salted caramel ice cream, berry cobbler, apple crumb cake, and gooseberry pie. All are amazing." She drew the last word out for emphasis. "What will it be?"

"I can't eat another bite, Zane."

"We'll just take the check. Everything was delicious."

Slight disappointment tinged the waitress's reply. "I'll get it right to you, sir."

He stretched out his arm, taking Sarah's hand in his, the same as he'd done during the entire ride to Missoula. It had been a wonderful drive, ending at a rustic, ranch-style restaurant on the edge of the city.

"If you don't mind, I want to stop at a horse tack and rodeo gear store next." He slid his chair a few inches closer.

"Fine with me. Do you think we'll have time to visit the historical museum at Fort Missoula?"

He squeezed her hand. "We have plenty of time. Anywhere else you want to go?"

"I wouldn't mind stopping by the Missoula Western Wear store. Beth said it's a great place to buy shirts."

"Works for me. I could use a couple more work shirts and another pair of Wranglers."

They stopped at the museum first, spending an hour before deciding to return soon. The tack and rodeo gear store was a ten minute drive.

Parking, Zane took Sarah's hand. As they walked up the steps, his attention landed on the driver of a gray sedan, who had a striking resemblance to the man he'd seen at the lake. Steps faltering, he rushed Sarah inside, suggesting they start at the back of the store.

While she looked through a large selection of antique tack, he made his way to the front door as the man exited the car. He wore the same khaki slacks and a similar shirt, though this one was black. Slipping his phone from a pocket, he took a few shots of the man and his car, including the license plate.

Zane continued watching as the man walked to his truck and glanced inside. He didn't seem interested in following them inside or approaching them. Was he watching him or Sarah? Why would he be interested in either one of them? There was one way to find out.

Checking behind him, he saw Sarah holding up a pair of vintage saddlebags. Her interest in old tack and equipment might give him time.

While the man still occupied himself by looking inside the truck, Zane walked out the door, moving straight toward him. Boots crunching on the gravel parking lot, the man whirled around. It wasn't soon enough.

Grabbing the stranger with both hands, Zane shoved him against the truck. Tugging his arms behind him, he used his body to hold him in place, growling into his ear.

"Who the hell are you, and why are you following us?"

"I don't know what you're talking about," he growled.

Glancing around, Zane noticed a couple leave the store. Too engrossed in their own conversation, they didn't look their way.

"You were at the ranch, then the lake. Now you're in Missoula. Tell me your name, and why you're so interested in us."

He didn't respond.

Irritated, Zane held the man's wrists in one hand while the other checked for identification. Nothing except a few dollars and spare change. Most importantly, no weapon. Bending down, he growled in the man's ear.

"My guess is you know something about me. Know what I'm capable of, so you're a member of one of our country's illustrious alphabet agencies. Which one, I don't know, but I can find out. Now, I have no desire to create problems for either of us, so here's the deal. Stay out of my life and Sarah's. Don't follow us again. If I spot you, which I will, I won't be so nice the next time. Do you get me?"

A few seconds passed before the man responded. "Yeah, I get you."

"Excellent." Turning the man around, Zane dropped his hands. "I don't expect to see you again." Heading back to the shop, he hesitated by the entrance to confirm the man had left. Zane wasn't disappointed.

Spotting Sarah holding up an old pair of chaps, he smiled. No way he'd let the man ruin the day with his girl.

His girl. Was Sarah his girl? A scary revelation assailed him, realizing he did want her to be his.

"Do you think these will fit me?" She held the chaps out to him.

"If not, you can always hang them on the wall."

Slapping him in the arm, she laughed. "Probably don't need them."

"The saddlebags you had earlier would be a better purchase. Where are they?"

"You saw me looking at them?"

"Obviously. Now, show them to me."

Ten minutes later, they walked out of the shop with Sarah's vintage saddlebags. In good condition, he guessed them to be from sometime between 1930 and 1940.

Lightning flashed across the sky to the south, followed seconds later by thunder. An unexpected downpour hit them several feet from the truck, prompting Sarah to hop inside while Zane ran to the driver's door. By the time he joined her, he was soaked.

Sarah held her sides, laughing. He didn't know if he'd ever seen a prettier sight. Wrapping an arm around her waist, he tugged her to him, moving wet strands of hair from her face. Giving her time to pull away, he lowered his head, covering her mouth with his.

What started as a slow, short kiss, deepened as his tongue explored the recesses of her mouth. Feeling her arm wrap around his neck, he tugged her closer as his hand moved up and down her back. She felt good against him. Too good for being in a public lot in the middle of the afternoon.

Taking his time ending the kiss, he brushed his lips across her brow before shifting away.

"Well..." she breathed out. "That was a nice surprise."

It was his turn to laugh. "There's more to come."

"I hope so." Her face had turned a glorious dark pink color. "So, where to next?"

The rain continued to pound, creating rivers of water to stream across the pavement. Zane gazed across the shopping center, his face brightening as a smile appeared. Starting the engine, he drove toward the sign which caught his attention.

"Where are we going?" She clipped on her seat belt, expecting a long drive. It didn't happen.

In less than a minute, he parked again. "I'll come around to your side. We'll have to run."

The question on her lips died when he exited the truck and rushed toward her side. They didn't have far to run. She estimated it to be less than fifty feet. How wet could they get?

"I'm soaked." Wringing out her hair with both hands, Sarah looked down at her soaked blouse and slacks. The outline of her bra was clearly visible through the now almost transparent cotton shirt. "I should go back for my windbreaker."

Putting an arm around her, Zane drew her to his side. "I'll get you something in there." He nodded toward the double doors.

Once inside, she looked around the cavernous interior. "It's a bowling alley. We're going bowling?"

"Unless you'd rather not."

"I'd love to bowl, although I'm not very good."

Taking her hand, he led her to a small shop selling shoes, socks, tops, sweatshirts, and various sundries. A round rack held a variety of men's and women's tops. Guessing her size, he held up a couple, one red, the other dark blue.

"Would either of these work?"

Taking the red one from his hand, she held it up. "This one."

"What about pants?"

"Mine didn't get as wet as my blouse. The top is fine. Oh, I left my purse in the truck."

"No problem. I've got this."

"I told you I wasn't very good." Sarah smiled as she removed her bowling shoes. "No matter what I try, I can't seem to get a strike."

"You got a couple."

"In three games. You're very good. Did you grow up playing?" Standing, she grabbed the bag holding her still damp shirt.

Zane thought back, wondering how much to tell her. Now wasn't the time to discuss his relationship with Debbie. It would lead to explaining her death, a topic not on the agenda for today.

"Friends and I played when we could. All of us were in high school, and lived on ranches. We'd play late, after chores and dinner. It didn't take long before our skills improved. When did you bowl?"

Thinking, her mouth screwed into a frown before she grinned. "I believe this is my third time."

Brows rising, Zane barked out a laugh. "You only played twice before today?"

"I'm pretty sure that's right."

"We'll have to fix that. Can't have my girl getting so many gutter balls." Settling an arm over her shoulders, he guided them outside, missing the look of surprise on Sarah's face. "I'm starving. Let's eat before driving back. What sounds good?"

His comment about being his girl still rolled around in her head, keeping her from answering. Was he saying she was his girlfriend? Did she consider him her boyfriend?

"Sarah?"

"Sorry. What did you say?"

"Dinner. What sounds good?"

"Steak and salad."

Brushing his lips over hers, he headed to the truck, checking for the man who'd followed them. He'd sent the images and license number to a friend who was a wizard with tracking people. Zane could've waited to check the guy out after they got home, but he was anxious to discover anything his friend could dig up.

"Sounds perfect. Kell and I've eaten at a steakhouse on the other side of town."

The conversation slowed as he drove, his mind on the man who'd been following them. His phone rang as they pulled into a parking space. Seeing the name, Zane answered.

"It's Talbot."

"Nothing. Face recognition brought back nothing conclusive. The license matches a rental car."

"Name of the driver?" Zane asked.

"John Smith. Real creative, huh? The address he gave is also bogus. Whoever he is, he knows how to cover his tracks."

Opening his door, Zane walked around to Sarah's side. He held off opening her door. "Which tells me he's government."

"That's my guess. What have you done lately to catch their attention?"

"Nothing." Opening the door, he reached out his hand to Sarah.

"Don't know what to tell you, man. If you get anything else that will help, let me know."

“I will. Thanks.” Ending the call, Zane pocketed his phone.

“Bad news?” Sarah asked as his fingers laced with hers.

“More like no news. It’s not a big deal, Sarah.”

Yet Zane knew it was.

Chapter Sixteen

"Come on, sweetheart." Zane placed a hand on Sarah's shoulder, jostling it lightly.

They'd spent almost three hours at the steakhouse, talking about her studies and goals, the ranch's breeding program, and early success of the boarding business. The conversation continued for half the journey home until Sarah had fallen asleep.

Zane didn't mind the quiet. He had a great deal to think about, not the least of which was his relationship with Sarah. Since losing Debbie, there'd never been a woman who caught and kept his attention...until Sarah.

Putting his finger on the reasons was a wasted effort. He simply enjoyed her company, thought of her when he rose each morning and before falling asleep at night. When together, he didn't want the time to end.

Grabbing the house key from her purse, he unlocked the front door before returning to the truck. "Sarah. You're home."

"Uh...huh."

Chuckling, Zane slipped his arms under her and lifted. She weighed nothing. Kicking the passenger door shut, he carried her inside and into her darkened bedroom. Without turning on a light, he placed Sarah on the bed, removing her sandals before drawing the spread over her.

Something strange, yet warm gripped his chest as he looked down on her. One other person had elicited such strong feelings, and she'd been gone a long time.

A fear unlike anything he'd experienced since Debbie died tore through him. This was why he'd avoided relationships. He couldn't take the chance, couldn't afford to put his heart out there a second time.

"Zane?"

Sarah's sleep roughened voice had him bending down to brush a kiss across her forehead. "I'll call you, sweetheart."

Her much smaller hand slipped into his. "Stay with me for a bit."

He shouldn't, yet he found himself sitting on the edge of the bed, keeping her hand tucked into his. Walking away, and not just from her bedroom, would be the wise choice. No one had ever accused him of being wise.

"Lay down and talk to me about something."

Running a finger down her cheek, he released a deep sigh. "You know I should go."

"Yes."

Glancing away, he tried to find the will to leave. Zane didn't know when he'd become so weak when around her. "What do you want me to talk about?"

She opened her mouth on a big, extended yawn. "Well...you could tell me how you and Kell met." Sarah shifted to give Zane room to stretch out.

Hesitating a moment before rolling onto his back, he laced his hands behind his head. Knowing he couldn't afford to sleep, he stilled when Sarah shifted against him, placing her head on his shoulder and a hand on his chest.

"Or you could tell me about your first love."

His breath caught at the thought of coming clean about what he and Debbie shared. He'd spoken of what happened once when the Macklins, Kell, and Beth gathered for dinner. Relaxed after a couple of drinks, he'd spilled the story. No one asked questions or brought it up again.

"Did Beth talk to you about it?"

She rubbed a circle on his chest with her hand. "No. She told me you never dated because of what happened to your fiancée."

"Then you already know the story." There was an edge to his voice. He began to rise, but subtle pressure from her hand had him staying in place.

"I'd never ask you to tell me the details of what happened. Tell me about your fiancée. What was she like?"

Unlacing his hands, he slipped an arm around her, holding her close. She'd been upfront with him about her boyfriends, bad choices, and regrets, asking nothing from him. Until tonight. Inhaling, he let out a slow, shaky breath. Maybe talking about her would help.

"We were in high school. Debbie was a new student, and the most gorgeous girl I'd ever seen. I couldn't believe it when we were assigned to the same work station for chemistry. She was shy, never talked much. Deb was also a good student and hard worker."

His hand moved up and down Sarah's arm as he collected his thoughts. "We began meeting for lunch and after school. I played football, and she came to watch my games. She was the sweetest person, with a heart as big as the sun. I fell hard, and so did she."

He recalled the first time they professed their love for each other. The memory still caused him pain.

"Debbie was on the softball team. She was real good. Played third base, and could hit any pitch. I loved watching her play. We both received scholarships to Montana State University. To celebrate, I took her out to the best place in town. That's when I proposed. I couldn't believe it when she accepted. The joy didn't last long."

He fell silent while continuing to move his hand up and down Sarah's arm. Leaning up, she pressed a kiss to his mouth.

"I'm so sorry you were hurt, Zane. So very sorry."

Not commenting, he tugged her closer. He was tired of talking. Tired of carrying Debbie's image in his head. Could replacing it with Sarah's beautiful face free his soul?

Zane blinked awake, not recognizing his surroundings. The soft body close to his brought back the events of the previous night. He remembered talking about him and Debbie, and Sarah's response.

"I'm so sorry you were hurt, Zane. So very sorry."

Glancing down at her, he was glad to see she was under the covers while he remained stretched out on the comforter. Careful not to wake her, he slid his arm out from under her before sitting up.

The clock on her dresser showed five in the morning. Hustling would get him back home in time to finish his chores. Zane didn't move from his spot on the edge of the bed.

Shifting, he ran a finger along Sarah's jaw, detouring down her smooth, ivory neck. The same warm sensation he'd felt before falling asleep assailed him. Lowering his head, he placed a soft kiss on her lips, hovering above her for a moment before pushing up and off the bed.

After a quick stop in the bathroom, he found a pad of paper and pen in the kitchen. Sprawling a quick note, he dashed outside and to his truck. Sunday had turned out to be one of the best days he'd experienced in ten years. It was all because of Sarah.

By the time he pulled onto the street, he already missed her. The sensation both surprised and disturbed him. He'd been telling himself a relationship didn't interest him. Yet here he was, revising his schedule in order to be with Sarah more often. Even working on his computer while she studied would be fine. Anything to stay close to her.

Shoving aside a persistent tug of apprehension, he accepted he wasn't ready to give Sarah up. What was the harm in seeing where their relationship would go? Yes, one or both of them could get hurt if it didn't work out. The opposite was also true.

"Slim chance," Zane muttered, parking close to the barn.

As he climbed out, Kell came out of the house with two cups of coffee, holding one out to him. "We've got a big day ahead of us."

"Yeah? What's happening?"

"The bank manager is coming out to check completion of the first stable, and review the plans for the second and third ones."

"Again? This will be the third time he's done the same." Zane blew across the top of the cup before taking a sip.

"Brent Nance has been promoted to district manager."

Leaning against the side of his truck. "When did this happen?"

"Friday. He's already in Billings. The new manager will be here in two hours."

"What's his name?"

"Ms. Karen Franklin."

Rubbing a hand across his brow, Zane shook his head. "Geez. Does she have any background in ranching?"

"Born near Helena. Grew up on the family ranch. Graduated from Montana State. Started with the Cattleman's Bank as a teller and was promoted up. Brent has assured me there won't be any issues."

"I've heard that before."

"True. But not about the ranch." Kell knew his friend referred to a mangled operation when they were still Army Rangers. "I'll get in touch with Brent if there are any hiccups."

"I'm counting on it. Suppose I should check the stalls, make sure the ranch hands have everything ready." Swallowing the last of the coffee, he handed the cup back to Kell.

"Long night?"

"What?" Zane hesitated saying more, knowing Kell already knew where he'd been. "Crashed at Sarah's. Nothing happened, so don't poke."

"You know I never poke." Kell chuckled.

"Don't say anything to Beth."

"Didn't plan to. Sarah will tell her about it anyway. She's come a long way from the party girl of her past."

Zane started toward the barn, then stopped, whirling back to face Kell. "She's special." His jaw worked as if he had more to say. Instead, he gave a slow shake of his head, shrugged, and turned away.

Sarah's eyes opened gradually. A memory from the night before had her rising to balance on an arm as she looked around. Zane was gone.

She'd woken about two in the morning, been surprised to find him still on top of the bed with an arm under her. He'd held her close, stroking her arm, never once trying to do more. It had been sweet, comforting.

Rolling out of bed, she padded to the bathroom. Thirty minutes later, showered, hair in a ponytail, and teeth brushed, she dressed for her shift at the nursing home.

Sarah checked the full-length mirror on the wall. She looked the same, though something significant had shifted over the last twenty-four hours. The same, yet different.

Inhaling the aroma of her morning coffee, she tied the comfortable loafers which made working at the nursing home tolerable. Pouring the only cup of coffee she'd have time to drink, her gaze scanned the kitchen.

On the counter, next to the refrigerator, was her pad of paper. Someone had written on the top sheet.

Moving closer, a small smile tipped her lips.

Thanks for the best night's sleep I've had in a very long time. When can I see you again? Tonight for dinner works for me. Text yes or no. Z.

A girlish chuckle burst from her lips. Grabbing her phone, she typed her response.

Yes.

Chapter Seventeen

Sarah finished a quick shower, spent almost no time drying her hair before applying moisturizer, blush, mascara, and a light topcoat of lip gloss. A text from Zane told her they were going to a casual place where t-shirts and jeans were the normal attire.

Slipping into her tightest pair, she selected a white t-shirt with ecru embroidery. She loved, though seldom wore, the top she'd purchased at a tiny boutique in Missoula. It had almost gone into a donation bag the previous summer. Looking in the mirror, Sarah was glad she'd given the top a reprieve.

Spending several more minutes using a large curling iron to add soft waves to her hair, she grabbed a dark blue swing sweater, which dropped to the same length as her shirt, and headed to the kitchen. Chamomile tea with honey would be perfect to calm her roiling stomach.

She'd felt off-kilter since realizing the depth of her feelings for Zane. The plan had been to have fun and stay detached. Instead, she'd fallen headfirst for the taciturn cowboy.

Leaning a hip against the counter, she sipped her tea, wondering if walking away now would be best. Her chest squeezed the instant the thought hit her heart. She didn't have time to ponder the situation further. Three raps on the front door signaled Zane had arrived.

Swallowing the last drops of tea, she placed the cup in the sink, noticing her hand shook ever so slightly. This was not good. Never had she felt such a strong wave of anticipation. Opening the door, the breath whooshed from her.

Zane stood erect in black jeans, which hugged his hips, a black t-shirt showcasing all his glorious muscles, and shiny, black boots. He held his black hat in one hand, an impish smile flashing when he saw her. Any woman who didn't find him attractive was blind.

"I thought you said casual." Stepping aside, she motioned him in.

Shrugging, he set the hat on a chair. "This is casual."

Before she could utter another word, he snaked an arm around her waist and kissed her. Sarah's hands moved up his arms and around his neck, drawing him down. This wasn't a brush of their lips. This was a full-on assault, causing warmth to flow through her. By the time he raised his head, they were both breathing hard. Seeing her glassy eyes, he grinned.

"You ready?"

Brushing a strand of hair from her face, she rocked on her heels. "Um...yes."

Picking up her sweater and a small, crossbody purse, she accepted the hand he offered. One more look around and they were out the door, heading to his truck.

"Where are we going?" She slid into the truck, setting her sweater and purse aside while Zane jogged around to the driver's side.

"There's a burger place south of Hamilton I've been wanting to try. Have you been to Lenny's?"

"Never heard of it. But I don't travel out of Whiskey Bend too often."

"Del's been there several times. Says they have the best burgers and sandwiches around."

"That's high praise considering how much he enjoys the burger place here in Whiskey Bend. I'm always willing to expand my knowledge."

Starting the engine, he looked at her. He loved the way Sarah was up for almost anything, saw new experiences as a way to learn something. Debbie hadn't been so adventurous. She'd always preferred going to the same places, and rarely ventured outside of town. Mentally chastising himself for thinking of Debbie while with Sarah, he headed out of Whiskey Bend.

Once on the highway, he reached over, taking her hand in his. "How was work today?"

"Same as always. Except we have a new resident. What a firecracker." Her eyes crinkled at the corners.

"How's that?"

"The woman's in her early sixties, acts as if she's twenty. Demanding, yet funny. She will make each day interesting."

"I didn't even consider you might have class tonight when I left the note. Are you skipping?"

"Not at all. The instructor took the day off for a family emergency. Gave us twice the homework for next week.

Nothing's ever free." A soft smile brightened her face, creating another tug on Zane's heart. "What about you?"

"We're asking for another release of approved loan funds. The new bank manager came by to check the place out. It seemed to go well." He turned off the highway and onto a two-lane road, which ended in a parking lot.

"I've met Brent Nance. Is he gone?"

"Promoted. A woman born and raised near Helena took over." Walking around the truck, he opened her door.

"How old is she?" She took his hand, sliding to the ground.

"I don't know. Maybe twenty-five or six."

"Pretty?"

He fell into an answer before thinking it through. "Very."

"Oh." The grip on his hand loosened, though she didn't let go.

"Not near as pretty as you, sweetheart." Opening the front door, he ushered her into an already crowded dining room. "A table for two, please."

The hostess led them across the room to what may have been the only booth left in the place. "Drinks?"

"Water for both of us to start." He waited for Sarah to slide in before slipping in beside her. Settling an arm over her shoulders, he bent down, kissing her. "Not even close to as beautiful as you," Zane whispered against her lips.

Feeling her face redden, she straightened away from him. Sarah had never been the jealous type. What was going on with her? Whatever it was, she didn't like it.

"I don't know why I asked about her." Looking down, she didn't meet his gaze, missing the humor in his eyes.

"It's natural. I'd have been curious if a guy about your age came by your house to check out the heater."

Snorting, she looked at him. "No, you wouldn't."

"Sure I would. A man doesn't want his woman hanging around handsome guys." Taking her chin between his thumb and index finger, he fixed her with a serious gaze before kissing her. "Make no mistake, Sarah. You *are* my girl."

Neither spoke much on the way back to Sarah's place. The food had been great, the service wonderful, yet she hadn't been able to get Zane's words out of her head.

"You are my girl."

The possessive tone of his voice didn't bother her. She felt the same about him. Did that mean they were a couple?

Parking in front of her house, he turned toward her. "Can I come in?"

"That would be nice. I do have to be at work early tomorrow, so I can't stay up late."

"Not a problem, sweetheart."

Inside, she made coffee for Zane and tea for herself before snuggling next to him on the sofa. "Do you want to watch a movie?"

"Depends. Does it have to be a chick flick?"

Chuckling, she shook her head. "It can be whatever you want. Well, except something scary. I want to be able to sleep tonight."

"All right then." Picking up the controller, he took his time, asking her thoughts before finally selecting one each would enjoy. An adventure comedy with a touch of romance.

The movie became a game of watching some scenes, kissing through others. By the time the closing credits ran on the screen, Zane knew, deep in his soul, he'd do all he could to keep Sarah in his life.

"Boone knows I can bring the supplies home. My guys load it for me, so it's not a problem." Willow Macklin tapped fingers on the feed store counter. "Anyway, that's not your problem, Zane."

Her words floated around him, comprehensible, yet not making much of an impact. After last night, he could think of little except Sarah and the way he felt when around her. The night before had been the sweetest thing Zane had ever experienced.

Sarah had fallen asleep against his chest. He'd held her for a long time, not wanting to break the connection. When she hadn't woken by midnight, he scooped her up and carried her to bed. It took him another ten minutes to talk himself into leaving.

The drive home had been cloaked in images of her, to the point he doubted sleep would come. It had been one of the most restful nights of his life.

"Zane, are you all right?"

"Yeah. Sorry." He shifted his body to lean against a display case in Robinson's Feed and Tack. The business passed down from her parents. "Look, Willow, Boone's protective, same as I'd be about a slip of a woman loading fifty pound bags of feed."

"Slip of a woman?" She snorted the question on a laugh. "I've worked here most of my life. The key to loading is leverage, and I've got that covered. Pull your truck up to the loading dock while I rustle up a couple guys."

"Will do." Lifting keys from his pocket, Zane headed for the door when someone caught his attention. Doing a double take, he couldn't stop staring at what he believed to be the same woman he'd seen driving the car at the ranch. The woman who looked so much like...

No, he wouldn't go there. Reminding himself everyone had a double somewhere in the world, he tore his eyes away.

Heading toward his truck, he scrubbed a hand over his face. On top of falling for a woman within weeks of first dating her, he now saw Debbie everywhere.

"Get yourself together, Zane." Maybe if he said it enough, he'd get over whatever caused the false sightings.

Debbie had been gone ten years. He'd been with her in the car that almost killed him. Seen her in the hospital. Held her hand as she took her last breath.

Maybe the confusion could be blamed on the fact he'd finally found someone else. He'd never believed a second chance at love would come his way. Hadn't put himself out there, or given any woman a chance to reach his heart.

Sarah was different. She came floating into his life through his friendship with Kell and Beth. He'd remembered her as a party girl, someone you'd hang with for a good time. The complete opposite of Debbie. Or that was what he'd thought.

She'd changed after deciding to become a teacher. He admired her work ethic and dedication to her goal.

Maybe it was because he was older, had more experience in the world, but this time around felt deeper, richer, than what he'd shared with Debbie. She'd always hold an important place in his heart. No longer would he allow her to own it at the exclusion of another woman.

Jumping into his truck, Zane didn't spare a glance at the woman. So what if she resembled his deceased fiancée?

Debbie was his past. He hoped Sarah would be his future.

Chapter Eighteen

Sheriff Del Macklin sat across from the mayor, a good friend of Mick Vogel, the attorney killed in the fiery crash at the gas station. Until today, he had nothing to report. Not a single reason to account for the deaths of Vogel and Belinda Graham, an attorney from Missoula.

"This is all conjecture, Del. You're relying on third party information, which, if correct, could taint a good friend and the woman with him." Jonathan Barnes had been Whiskey Bend's mayor for ten years, and had already decided to run again when this term ended.

"A third party who's reliable, Mayor. My source is ninety percent certain Mick and Belinda were working together to discredit the testimony of federal witnesses in the Maldonado Cartel conviction."

"Hired by the cartel to overturn the convictions?"

"That's my understanding."

"Because of this, they were killed?"

"Again, that's what my source claims." Del drummed his fingers on the table, waiting for the question he knew would come.

"Who is this source?"

Bingo, Del thought. "Sorry, Mayor. That information is confidential."

Jumping to his feet in classic Barnes's style. Pacing behind his chair, he rubbed the top of his head with a broad hand. "So your source is saying Mick and Belinda were working for the cartel. Sorry, but I don't see it. Mick might've been an obnoxious sod at times, but he wouldn't have agreed to work for an organization bringing millions of dollars of illegal drugs into the U.S. It just wouldn't have happened."

Del tended to agree. He and Mick were professional acquaintances, not friends. In the years he'd known the attorney, his practice centered on business, real estate, family, and estate planning law. Mick had never handled criminal cases.

"You may be right, but this is the information I'm getting from my source. I thought you'd want to know."

Mayor Barnes lowered himself into his large, leather executive chair, his face slack with disbelief. Rubbing his forehead, his lips formed a tight line.

"My source doesn't know who went after Mick," Del said. "Could be another cartel."

"Or someone from the government."

Del's brows lifted. "What do you mean?"

"The DEA spent years and a good deal of resources putting the Maldonado members away. They have a vested interest in not having the convictions overturned. If I recall correctly, some of the testimony came from a man the DEA placed in WITSEC." Barnes mentioned the witness protection program run by the U.S. Marshal Service.

Del nodded. "You're right. There were others, but his testimony and the video he took sealed their fate."

"If Mick and Belinda found evidence to discredit the witness..." Jonathon's voice trailed off.

"It would be a black mark on the DEA. The source speculated they may have been killed because there was proof the witness's testimony was corrupted. Although that scenario doesn't make sense to me. Why would anyone fabricate damaging information about the cartel? In my mind, only a lunatic would place themselves in such extraordinary danger."

Slapping his hands on the desk, the mayor stood. "I have a meeting to attend. Thanks for the update, Del. Let me know what else you learn."

"Will do." Dismissed, Del continued to mull over what his source told him as he walked to the sheriff's department building.

He understood the witness was no longer in WITSEC per se, though he and his family had been relocated with new identities. Del had gone through Mick's files after his death, finding nothing connecting him to the trial or the cartel. Nothing in his home, either.

Del had to consider the crash that killed Mick and Belinda was what it first appeared. An accident. Even excellent sources could be wrong.

Approaching Evie's Diner, the smell of onion rings and grilled burgers wafted to the sidewalk. On cue, his stomach growled, reminding him he hadn't eaten since an early breakfast. Glancing in the window, he spotted two friends wave at him, beckoning him inside.

Josh Reyes and Maggie O'Dell, one of his two detectives, sat at a table for four. They'd all been friends for years. Maggie's husband had died a couple years earlier when he'd hit a patch of ice on the highway, rolling down an embankment before slamming into a tree. She'd been slowly recovering the loss after an extended period of grieving. They'd been together since high school.

"Have you eaten?" Del took a seat at one of the chrome chairs with red vinyl seats.

Josh shook his head. "Just getting ready to order."

One of Evie's new waitresses appeared, bright eyed with a broad smile. "What can I get you?"

All three ordered burgers and drinks. Josh and Del added onion rings, and Maggie asked for fries. Not much had changed since they were teenagers.

"How are you, Josh?" Del took a sip of water while scanning the people in the diner. Similar to Wicked Waters at night, Evie's was the place locals frequented for lunch.

"Great. Business at the shop is up, keeping everyone busy. Thorn didn't join us because some hotshot from Seattle flew in to order bikes for him and his wife. They're hammering out the details. We have another high roller coming in this evening for the same. We're hiring more employees. Unfortunately, not many people in Whiskey Bend have the experience we require."

Del understood. On a few occasions, he'd helped out at Scorpion Custom Motorcycles, the shop owned by his brother, Thorn, Josh, and Tony Coletti. Their work was high-end, attracting those with funds to make their dream bike a reality.

"Where do you find the right people?" Maggie asked.

"One of our guys is from Seattle. Another from Huntington Beach in California. We pay for them to fly out on a Friday. They do some projects Saturday and Sunday, which gives us a chance to judge their work."

The waitress set down their drinks. "Food's about ready." She dashed off to check on another table before heading for the kitchen.

Josh picked up his soda, taking a long swallow. "So how is the investigation into the gas station crash going?"

Del's mouth twisted into a grimace. "It's going. Wish I could talk about it, but you know the rules."

Maggie sipped root beer through a straw, glancing toward Del. "Am I going to get involved in this one, boss?"

"I'm not sure yet. I'll tell you what I have when we get back to the station."

"Now that's just rude," Josh complained, resting an arm over the back of the chair next to him.

"Sorry, man. You want in, apply for a position."

A bark of laughter burst from Josh's throat. "Nope. I make too much money tinkering with motorcycles."

"Fair enough." Del took another look around the restaurant, his eyes locking on a man with a yellow polo shirt across the room. He'd seen him a few times around town in the last few weeks. Although he couldn't pinpoint the reason, something about the man put him on alert.

"Either of you know the man sitting alone at a table across the room. Yellow polo shirt."

"He stopped by the shop a week ago," Josh said. "Thorn spoke with him. That's all I know."

"What about you, Maggie?"

"I've seen him in here a couple times, but that's it, boss."

"Three burgers. Two with onion rings, one with fries." Setting plates down, the waitress grabbed ketchup from another table. "Anything else?"

"I think we're good. Thanks." Josh popped a small onion ring into his mouth before picking up his burger.

"You know what? I also saw him at the feed store when I stopped by to see Willow. He seemed to just be hanging around, which is what caught my attention." Maggie ate a french fry, her brows drawing together in concentration. "I don't think he bought anything. His attention was pinned on one of the new employees. Willow introduced her to me as Tamara. Pretty, with her long hair worn in a ponytail. It all seemed strange."

Swallowing down a bite of his burger with water, Del shot another look at the stranger. "I'll have to ask Willow about the new employee and our guy over there. Have either of you ever seen him with someone?"

"Not me," Maggie answered at the same time Josh shook his head.

Knowing nothing about the man, Del pegged him as law enforcement. Maybe it was the overall look and demeanor. Close cropped hair, rigid posture, the way he continually scanned the room with an expression Del would describe as wary. He couldn't help wondering why the man was in Whiskey Bend.

Tom Dekker sensed more than saw eyes on him. He'd always had terrific instincts, it was one of the characteristics which made his career in the U.S. Marshal Service so successful.

Sheriff Del Macklin had joined friends at a table near the front of the diner. Without looking, he'd lay odds the lawman watched him while eating his burger and onion rings, the same lunch Tom had just finished.

Evie's Diner had become his unofficial office while in Whiskey Bend. Excellent food, and the perfect place to meet the locals.

Finishing his coffee, Tom put money on the table and stood. His target had just taken his last bite of a burger. Making his way between tables, he stepped outside, taking a position several feet from the door. He didn't have to wait long. A few minutes later, Del left the diner.

"Sheriff Macklin?"

"Yes?"

"I'm Tom Dekker." He extended his hand, which Del accepted. "I wonder if you'd have a few minutes to meet with me."

"About?"

"I'd rather we talk in private. Wherever you want is fine with me."

"All right. Let's walk to my office. What agency are you with?"

Tom chuckled. "I'm that obvious?"

"Probably not to most people. It's my job to be aware of the new people in town. You've been here about two weeks."

"Two weeks and a couple days."

Del opened the main entrance door to the station, motioning for Tom to enter. "Who do you work for?"

"I'm a U.S. Marshal. I've taken a long-term leave of absence."

"To travel the country?" Del walked into his office, pointing to a chair.

Closing the door, Tom sat down. "In part. Just not in the way you may think."

Chapter Nineteen

"That's the way, Sarah. Lean back in the saddle and give the horse his head." Zane waited at the bottom of a steep, but short trail. "Relax and let the horse do the work."

The smile she bestowed on him when reining up next to his horse was a punch to his chest.

"I did it." She let out a long breath.

"You sure did, sweetheart. And you looked great doing it."

"Where to next?"

He'd invited her to the ranch for a late afternoon ride. They'd already been gone for almost an hour, and still had to turn back.

"Are you sure you're up for more?"

"Absolutely."

Zane studied her, not seeing the exhaustion he expected. The excitement in her expression helped make the decision.

"All right. Instead of circling back to the ranch, we'll take a little different route. More difficult, and it will take about fifteen minutes longer. What do you think?"

"I'm ready."

"Let's go."

Riding a winding trail along the edge of the national forest, they arrived at the ranch ninety minutes later. The long, summer day had finally given way to darkness as they groomed the horses and secured them in large stalls.

"That was wonderful. Thanks for inviting me."

Wrapping his arms around her, he drew her close. Covering her mouth with his, he tightened his hold when her hands clasped behind his neck. Aligning her body against his, one broad hand moved down her spine, resting on the swell of her hips. In no hurry, he ravished her mouth, wanting more, knowing now wasn't the time, and definitely not the place.

Footfalls on the hard dirt confirmed his thoughts. Raising his head, he placed a last kiss on her forehead as Kell stopped near them.

Nodding at Sarah, he looked at Zane. "Sorry to interrupt, but Beth sent me to tell you she saved dinner for you. It's wrapped and keeping warm in the oven. Also, Rona Kessler came by while you were gone. She asked for you."

On a groan, he put a small amount of distance between himself and Sarah, threading his fingers through hers. "Did she say what she wanted?"

"Nope. I didn't get the impression it was about her horses." Kell's mouth twisted into a sympathetic grin. "I told her you'd call."

Sensing Sarah's gaze on him, Zane tightened his hold on her hand. "I'll do that tomorrow."

Turning to leave, Kell walked several feet before looking over his shoulder. "The woman's unrelenting."

"You have no idea."

"Who's Rona?"

Zane had expected Sarah's question. Grimacing, he stroked the palm of her hand with his thumb.

"She boards four horses with us."

"And she has an interest in you."

"I don't know what the woman wants. The important thing is I have absolutely no interest in her." He looked down at Sarah as they walked through the back door into the kitchen. "Are you happy with how things are between us?"

Blinking a couple times, she nodded. "Yes."

"Well, so am I." Releasing her hand, he opened the oven door. Grabbing potholders, Zane removed a nine by thirteen glass dish from the oven, placing it on a trivet by the stove. Removing the foil on top, he inhaled. "You up for chicken casserole?"

"Are you kidding? I'm starving, and Beth makes the best casseroles. I'll get plates. What do you want to drink?"

"Water for me."

They were slipping forkfuls of noodles, chicken, and vegetables into their mouths within minutes. Cleaning his plate, Zane scooped up another serving, offering more to Sarah, who shook her head.

Finishing, she pushed the clean plate away and leaned back in her chair. "I can't eat another bite. That was perfect." Standing, she picked up her glass. "Do you want more water?"

"Please."

“There’s a cherry pie in the keeper.” Beth entered the kitchen, lifting a plastic container from a cupboard.

“I’m stuffed. How about you, Zane? I’ll bet there’s ice cream, too.” Sarah lifted a brow, smiling.

“Pie and ice cream sounds great.”

“How was the ride?” Beth dragged a chair away from the table, taking a seat while Sarah warmed up a slice of pie for Zane.

“Great. I could’ve stayed out longer, but it was getting dark.” Adding ice cream to the plate, Sarah set it down in front of Zane.

“You’re gonna be sore tomorrow,” he said, scooping pie into his mouth.

Beth stood at the knock on the front door. Walking through the kitchen and across the living room, she looked through the peephole.

“Del. What a nice surprise.” She glanced around him. “Is Amy with you?”

“At home.”

“Come in. Zane and Sarah were just finishing dinner after a late ride. Have you eaten?”

“Grabbed a burger on my way over. Evening, Zane, Sarah.” He accepted Zane’s outstretched hand.

Beth pulled out a chair. “Sit down, Del. Can I get you something to drink?”

“I’m good. Thanks.” Mouth drawing into a tight line, he met Zane’s gaze. “Do you have a few minutes?”

“Sure.”

“In private.”

"Um, yeah."

"Kell headed out to the barn a little bit ago. You can use his office."

Del pushed back his chair. "Thanks, Beth."

Brushing a kiss across Sarah's cheek, he followed Del to the office down the hall. "What's going on?"

Closing the door behind them, Del motioned toward a couple of chairs. "Seems you and Sarah are doing good."

"Real good. But that's not what you want to talk about, right?"

"No, it's not." Jaw tight, he seemed to be mulling over what to say.

"Just spit it out, Del."

"It's not that simple, man." Rubbing his brow, he blew out a slow breath. "Have you noticed a guy in town who looks like he might be a fed?"

"Short hair, polo shirts, and khaki pants?"

"That's the one. He thought you'd made him."

"Not hard when he followed Sarah and me to Missoula. So you know this guy?"

"Just met him today. His name's Tom Dekker. He's a U.S. Marshal on a leave of absence."

"Okay. Why's he in Whiskey Bend?"

"It's a little complicated, so let me get it out before you react. Agreed?"

Zane's brows drew together as his mouth twisted in question. "I'll do my best."

"There's a woman named Tamara O'Dell. She moved to town about two months ago, is working for Willow at the feed store. You knew her as Debbie Wilson."

"What?" Zane shot to his feet. "That's not possible. She died in a car crash. I went to her funeral."

Del held up both hands, palms out. "I know, man. This is going to be tough to hear, but you need to let me explain."

Pacing across the room, he whirled back toward Del. "Where is she?"

"I'll get to that."

Shoving both hands through his hair, he forced himself to sit down. "Fine. Explain it."

"Debbie spent most of her youth in a middle-class neighborhood outside of Dallas. Her father and Rona's—"

"Rona?"

"Rona Kessler."

Zane whispered something Del couldn't hear before motioning for him to continue.

"Their fathers knew each other since elementary school. Stayed friends, even though the Kesslers and Debbie's family were at distinct ends of the financial and social circles. When Debbie was fourteen, both parents lost their jobs. They sold their house and moved away from Dallas. The family moved several times over the years as they chased jobs. At least, that's the unofficial story."

Zane's back straightened, his eyes flickering with renewed interest. "What's the truth?"

"Debbie's father worked construction. Was a supervisor for a large outfit in Denver. Seems he witnessed something he shouldn't have."

"What?"

"The murder of three men by the Maldonado Cartel."

Zane's nostrils flared and jaw worked, but he didn't comment.

"He went to the police."

"That was mistake number one."

"Appears so. Maldonado had several police on his payroll. Someone tried to run him off the road, shot up his truck. He went to the FBI. Long story short, the family ended up in WITSEC."

"Witness protection?"

"Yeah. The cartel found them, so they moved around several times. That's how you met Debbie. According to Tom Dekker, the U.S. Marshal, Debbie refused to leave when they found the family in your hometown. She didn't want to leave you. Her parents forced her into going with them."

"Debbie died in the accident. I saw her, Del. I saw…" His voice trailed off as he saw the truth on Del's face.

"Dekker told me you were unconscious from the wreck. You never actually saw her after the truck ran into you. It was a ruse, Zane. They were sent to South Dakota."

Zane's gaze latched onto a spot on the carpet, his body refusing to move. His breaths were short intakes and exhales. Chest tight, his muscles froze in place. Nothing in his training had prepared him for this level of truth. For Debbie being alive.

"She wants to see you. According to Dekker, well…" Del let out a sigh. "What do you want me to tell Dekker?"

Zane forced normal breaths, regulating the heart pounding in his chest.

Debbie hadn't died that day. She'd been alive all these years while he grieved for a death, and a dream, which never happened.

Standing, he walked on leaden legs across the room to an open window. Staring outside, he cleared his throat before turning back to stare at Del.

"Tell Dekker I want to see her."

Chapter Twenty

Sarah hadn't moved from her spot at the table next to Beth, drinking coffee, talking, and waiting. Zane and Del had been in the office a long time. Much longer than she'd imagined when they left the room. Kell didn't join them, preferring to watch baseball and read.

"What do you think they're talking about, Beth?"

"I have no idea. It's unusual for Del to come over without Amy, which makes this stranger than it already is."

"I've got work in the morning, so I can't stay too much longer." At the sound of men's voices, Sarah shifted to see Del and Zane coming down the hall. Instead of looking her way, the two walked straight out the front door. "Zane?"

Slowing his pace, he glanced at her. His eyes narrowed a moment before he gave a slow shake of his head and continued outside. Taking a few tentative steps forward, she picked up her pace at the sound of an engine starting.

"Where would they be going?"

Beth shook her head. "I have no idea, but it must be serious."

"Since I don't know how long Zane will be gone, I'm going to head home. Will you let him know?"

"Sure."

Walking Sarah outside, she waited as the engine started. "Drive safe." Waving as she drove toward the road, Beth couldn't help an odd sense of foreboding from lodging in her stomach.

Sarah concentrated on the road ahead, trying not to read too much into Zane's odd behavior. He'd been so attentive during their ride and through dinner. The meeting with Del had changed something. The not knowing ate at her.

Turning toward town, she saw two cars in the parking area of Willow's feed store. One was Del's. Pulling in at the far end, she turned off the engine, as well as her lights. Sarah didn't feel any shame at watching.

Zane and Del climbed out, but didn't move toward the other cars. Rolling down her window, she could hear the two men talking, but couldn't make out the words.

Several minutes passed before a man emerged from the other car. Sarah couldn't be positive, but he looked like the man they'd seen in Missoula.

From the other side of the car, a woman she didn't recognize got out. Sarah's gaze moved to Zane, who stared at the woman before he began walking toward her.

Sarah's heart began to pound when the woman moved toward Zane, picking up her pace the closer she got. The woman stopped a foot away, staring up at him before jumping into his open arms.

Sarah didn't know how long they embraced, but when they pulled back, Zane cupped the woman's face and kissed her. Even from fifty yards away, Sarah could see tears streaming down the woman's face.

Feeling as if her world had imploded, Sarah felt her body begin to pulse, her own tears beginning to fall.

"You shouldn't be here."

Startled, Sarah spun around to see Del leaning against her car.

"You're right." When she started to climb into the car, Del grabbed her arm.

"Sarah, wait. You don't even know what's going on."

"I don't have to know what's going on to see what's happening." She looked down at his hand on her arm until he loosened his grip and stepped away.

"I'll let him know you were here."

"Please don't." Rolling up the window, she drove away, swiping at the continued stream of tears.

She'd been such a fool. How did she not know there was another woman in his life? Well, maybe not in Whiskey Bend. It appeared they'd been separated from each other for a while. Where did she live, and why was Del involved? Did it matter?

"No," she whispered to herself. Nothing about Zane Talbot mattered anymore.

Parking in the driveway of her small home, Sarah turned off the engine, but didn't move. Staring straight ahead, she couldn't summon the energy to enter the house. Loneliness engulfed her. Before Zane, she'd been alone, although not often lonely. She didn't need a therapist to realize something precious had died tonight.

Men had come and gone over the years. She hadn't been in love with any of them. The gaping hole in her heart told a truth she didn't want to admit. She'd fallen hard for Zane Talbot. He was the first man who'd captured her heart. The first to break it.

"You're a big girl, Sarah. This pain will soon pass, and you'll forget him." If she said it enough, maybe she'd begin to believe it.

Zane stared into almond shaped blue eyes, the same ones he saw in his dreams. Debbie was alive, standing before him, looking more beautiful than he remembered.

"I can't believe you're here." Cupping her face, he kissed her again.

"You can believe it, Zane. I'm here, and I'm not leaving you again."

"Janelle?"

Both turned at the man's voice. "Yes, Tom?"

"We should get you back to your place. You never know who might be watching."

"As always, you worry too much. Besides, I just found Zane again."

"I'll have Del drive us back to Kell's place. We can talk before I take you home." He looked at the marshal. "Will that work for you, Tom?"

"I'll follow you to the Brooks's home."

She shook her head. "You don't have to do that, Tom. I'll be safe with Zane. Go home and get some sleep. You deserve it."

"All right. But I'll come by your place in the morning."

"Fine. Then you can follow me to work." She smiled up at Zane. "He's my guardian angel. Has been since I was fourteen."

"If you're sure."

"Go on, Tom. Zane and I need time to talk."

"Call if you need anything."

"You know I will."

They waited until Tom drove off before walking toward Del. "Can you give us a ride back to Kell's?" Zane looked down, realizing he'd taken her hand.

It was then he remembered Sarah, how he'd left her without a word. An odd pain sliced through him. What was he going to do about Sarah?

"Get in. I need to get back to Amy."

Something on Del's face and in his voice bothered Zane. Had he already thought of Sarah, wondering what was going to happen when another woman showed up at Kell's?

Zane had never felt so conflicted. The last thing he wanted to do was hurt Sarah. He cared a great deal about her. But with Debbie back...

Del dropped them off at Kell's, not getting out. He'd said nothing during the drive, which further bothered Zane. Something was definitely off.

He didn't hold Debbie's hand when they entered the house, wanting to speak to Sarah first. To his surprise, the house was almost dark, with no sign of Sarah. Looking out the front window, he noticed her car was gone.

"Sit down. I'll get us some water." Grabbing a couple bottles, he joined her on the sofa. "Is your real name Janelle?"

"Yes. Janelle Jensen." She took a long swallow of water, holding the bottle with a shaky hand. "I've been nervous all day, knowing we'd be meeting soon."

"Why didn't you come to me yourself? I've seen you several times around town and once at the ranch. You could've said something any of those times."

She waved him off, as if his questions were ridiculous. "Maybe I wasn't ready."

"But you were ready today?" He studied her, wondering if the Debbie he remembered was inside Janelle.

"Tom believed the time was right. Besides, he'll go back to the U.S. Marshal Service soon, and he wanted to make sure I wasn't alone."

Zane found her answer baffling. "I don't understand."

"Did the sheriff tell you about me being in WITSEC?"

"Yes. At least part of it."

"Well, Tom believes the Maldonado Cartel has sent men after me, even though I know nothing of what my father witnessed. Nor can I change the fact his testimony sent some of their men to prison. So, I continue to move around, not allowing myself to stay in one town too long.

With him leaving soon, Tom wanted to make sure we were back together. He believes you can protect me."

Resting an arm on the back of the sofa, he took in her words. They weren't reassuring. "What are your feelings for me, Janelle?"

Shrugging, she tucked both legs under her. "Of course I still love you, Zane. It's no different than in high school."

Her answer didn't comfort him. "It's been ten years. I've changed a great deal in that time. I'm certain you have changed, too."

"Well, I've gotten older. Does it really matter? Can't we just start up where we left off?"

The more he heard, the less Zane could see the woman he loved years ago in the woman sitting next to him. Still, he owed it to both of them to see if there was any chance of a future together.

Again, he thought of Sarah, and his heart squeezed. He recalled how not long ago he'd told himself Janelle was his past, Sarah his future.

Scooting toward him, she wrapped her arms around his neck. He allowed her to draw him closer. They kissed. Maybe it was all the questions in his head, or the surprise at seeing her after all these years, but the kiss didn't affect him the way it should. Not the way it had in the parking lot.

Yet he couldn't walk away. For ten years, he'd grieved her, believed her dead. He needed answers, and Janelle was the only one who could provide them.

Gently disengaging her arms from his neck, he dropped a kiss on her cheek before tucking her under his chin. They sat in silence for several minutes.

She didn't quite feel the same against his side. More stiff than he remembered.

"Tell me where you've been the last ten years."

Janelle was quiet for so long he didn't think she'd answer. When she spoke, the words were stilted, as if she'd memorized them from a script.

"Here and there."

"Where did you go after the fake crash?"

Stiffening a little more, she moved away, clasping her hands in her lap. "Father found a job in Oregon, so we moved to Hillsboro. That lasted a year before we moved again. This time to Colorado, not far from Denver. After that, we moved to Kansas, then back to Oregon."

"Why so many moves?"

"Tom said the cartel had learned of our location. Father believed Mother used to sneak off and call her sister. She denied it, but I agreed with him. So did Tom. She'd go shopping, buy a burner phone, call her sister, then toss it. She finally confessed when we returned to Oregon after living in Kansas."

"Where were you when they died?"

"Oregon. I stayed for a while, then started moving around. The feds provided protection for several months before removing me from the program. Father had already testified and the cartel members were in jail, so why continue providing resources to protect me? The decision was fine with me. There were places I wanted to see without them dictating where I had to live. I've been traveling around ever since."

"Is it how you see your future?"

"Maybe." She giggled. "It all depends on how we work out, Zane." Snuggling back against him, she sighed at the same time he grimaced.

Ten years had changed her more than a little.

Chapter Twenty-One

Sleep had never graced Zane after he'd taken Janelle home. They'd kissed briefly before she disappeared inside. He'd stood on the front porch for a minute, staring at the closed door while trying to figure out what had him so unsettled.

Zane didn't really need to wonder. He knew. The Janelle of today wasn't the woman he remembered from high school.

Hands clasped behind his head, he stared at the bedroom ceiling, wide awake, and knowing sleep wouldn't come. Too much had happened in the past twenty-four hours.

His initial excitement at having her back had faded as they'd talked. The outside was the same. Strawberry blonde hair, blue eyes, and creamy skin devoid of blemishes. Inside was where he felt the disconnect.

Their conversations ten years ago were genuine, full of real emotion. They were linked in a way he'd never experienced again until Sarah.

"Sarah," he muttered, wishing this was something he could talk through with her.

He wondered how long she'd waited with Beth before giving up on his return to the house and drove home. Zane knew she'd have questions. How would he answer?

Glancing at the clock, he winced. Five in the morning.

Tired of lying there seeking answers which wouldn't come, he threw off the covers, leaving the warmth of his bed. Ten minutes later, face washed, teeth brushed, and dressed, he headed downstairs to the kitchen.

The single serving coffeepot was warmed up and ready to go. Leaning against the counter as his dark roast Sumatra dripped into a cup, he found himself thinking about Sarah.

Recalling her schedule, she'd work an eight hour shift, head home to eat, then drive to the community college for class. He could catch her at home while she ate. Maybe he'd call, ask about stopping by her house before she left for school. What would he say?

Honesty was always best. Telling her Debbie had showed up, alive and well, would certainly generate questions. How would he answer?

"Morning." Beth joined him, pulling a cup from the cupboard. Dressed in lightweight jogging pants and a t-shirt, he knew she'd be heading out for her morning run.

"Morning." Sipping his coffee, he watched as she stretched arms above her head, then bent to touch her toes. When finished, she studied him. "What?"

"I'm wondering if you've spoken to Sarah since you drove off last night."

"Not yet. Why?"

"You'll want to speak with her. Today, if possible." Walking to the front door, she stopped to look back at Zane, a question in her expression. Instead of voicing it, she stepped outside to begin her run.

Kell walked into the kitchen a moment later, going straight to the coffeepot. "Zane."

"Morning." Sipping his now cool liquid, he waited as his friend's coffee brewed.

Picking up the cup, Kell leaned against the counter a couple feet away from Zane. "One of the ranch hands quit yesterday. He accepted a job in Wyoming. Willow's going to post it at the feed store. I've also placed an ad on the internet site we use."

"I'd planned to work with the men today, so we should be fine. I'll get started." Rinsing his cup, he set it in the sink.

"Zane?"

"Yeah?"

"Whatever happens, be careful with Sarah." Kell drank the last of his coffee, set his cup next to Zane's, and walked past him to the back door.

Watching Kell head toward the barn under construction, he let out a pent-up breath. First, Beth telling him to call Sarah, then Kell warning him to be careful. Those were tagged onto Del's odd behavior the night before, and Zane's own misgivings about rekindling anything with Janelle.

He'd be a fool not to pay attention to the subtle warnings from his friends. Adding his own doubts, he vowed to be careful with both Janelle and Sarah.

Stalking out of the house, he joined the other ranch hands in the barn. Seeing they were almost finished mucking the stalls, he began tossing flakes of hay into the feed bins of each stall.

Finishing, he checked the plastic containers of bags filled with supplements. Provided by the horse owners, the ranch hands emptied them into smaller bins used for this purpose.

He walked through the barn, spotting nothing warranting his or Kell's attention. After talking to one of the ranch hands, Zane headed toward the second barn. About a quarter of the way finished, they already had a long waiting list. Construction would commence on barn three within the next month.

Pulling out his phone, he checked the time. Sarah should be getting ready for work. Hitting speed dial, he waited through eight rings and her answering message.

"Sarah, it's Zane. Call me when you have a chance. If you have time, I'll pick up food for a quick dinner between your work and class. Let me know."

Sliding the phone back into his pocket, he expected to hear from her within a few minutes. Four hours later, there'd been no return call or text.

He'd left two more messages in the early afternoon. When Zane hadn't heard from her by three that afternoon, he called Del. "I wanted to thank you for last night."

"I was just the messenger."

"Tell me what was bothering you when we drove back to Kell's."

There was a pause before Del responded. "All right. Sarah was at the parking lot last night. She saw you and Janelle."

Zane's heart skipped a beat as he recalled his reunion with Janelle. "All of it?"

"Most. According to Beth, she was on her way home and saw my car in the parking lot. I spoke with her before she drove off."

"How was she?"

"How do you expect? She was upset, Zane."

"She won't return my calls."

"Do you blame her?"

Swallowing a painful ball of regret, he glanced toward the barn, seeing Kell walking toward him. "I have to go. Thanks for letting me know."

"Don't hurt her any further, Zane. She's part of the family." Del ended the call before he could respond.

Kell stopped beside him. "You look like someone kicked your puppy."

Rubbing his face, Zane looked at the ground. "More like I kicked the puppy."

"Let me guess. The puppy is Sarah."

Zane gave a slow nod.

"Sarah called Beth late last night. Told her what she saw. Said it was over between the two of you. Have you spoken with her today?"

"She won't respond to my voice messages or texts. I'm going to get some takeout and head over to her house. I hope to catch her between work and school."

"Are you and...what's her name?"

"Janelle's her real name."

"Are you planning to make a go of it with Janelle?"

"I don't know, Kell. My feelings for Sarah are strong. The little time I've spent with Janelle tells me she's nothing like the woman I fell in love with ten years ago." Rubbing the back of his neck, he looked toward the house. "If you don't mind, I'm going to clean up and drive over to Sarah's."

Kell clasped a hand on Zane's shoulder. "Go. Make things right with your lady."

One of the many thunderstorms common to Montana busted loose as Zane left the house. Hard rain pelleted the truck, forcing him to turn the wipers to high and slow his speed.

Turning toward town, he drove through the drive-up of the Mexican food restaurant Sarah preferred. Chicken tacos and an order of churros were her favorite. He was back on the road in minutes, once again navigating in the torrential downpour.

Thinking through what he planned to say to Sarah, he hit his left blinker, waiting as a truck went through the intersection. Pressing on the accelerator, he'd almost completed his turn when something broadsided him, sending the truck into a spin.

Turning the wheel into the spin, he'd almost straightened the truck when he was slammed from behind. The impact pushed the truck off the road, down an embankment, and into a roll. The last thing Zane saw was a cement wall before everything went black.

Sarah sat in the waiting room with Beth, Kell, and Del. The sheriff, soaking wet, with rips in his pants and shirt, stood near a window, looking out on the continuing storm. He'd been the one to call Kell, explaining what he'd seen when they all met in the surgery waiting room.

Del and one of his deputies had witnessed the accident, been the first on the scene. The sheriff had recognized the truck right away.

Bringing his SUV to a skidding stop, he'd ran down the embankment while the deputy called an ambulance. Slipping more than once, Del had stopped at the truck, peering inside to see an unconscious Zane, blood running down his face.

"I couldn't get to him until the paramedics arrived. Worst feeling of being helpless when a good friend may be taking his last breaths." Leaving his spot by the window, Del lowered himself into a chair next to Kell, burying his face in both hands.

"You did everything you could." Kell clasped Del's shoulder. "You have to be positive. The surgery will go fine, and Zane will be back at the ranch in no time."

Del lifted a brow. "You believe that?"

"Have to. The alternative isn't acceptable."

Sarah listened to their conversation, praying Kell was right. She'd been told Zane was on his way to her house when someone ran him off the road. Neither Del nor his deputy had been close enough to get a license number, or even the make and model of the vehicle responsible for Zane's truck rolling down the embankment.

She'd considered staying at home when Beth called, letting her cousin and Kell sit in vigil at the hospital. No matter what happened between Zane and the woman from his past, Sarah couldn't wait at home.

The doors to the surgery opened, allowing a female doctor to step into the room. "Family of Zane Talbot?"

"That's us." Kell stood before offering his hand to help Beth up.

"He came through surgery great. Most of the injuries were minor. A sprained wrist, abrasions and contusions on his arms and legs. We completed surgery on his ruptured spleen, requiring the removal of a portion of it. This was a much better solution, as it lessens the chance of infection. The worst was the injury to his head. We'll keep him under observation for several days to determine if TBI occurred."

"Traumatic brain injury?" Del asked.

"Yes. We'll be performing additional tests to determine the extent of damage. He is concussed, which is always a concern."

"When can we see him?" Kell squeezed Beth's hand.

"Mr. Talbot has been moved to recovery. A nurse will let you know when he's ready for visitors. Any questions?"

Sarah stepped forward. "When do you believe he can go home?"

"It's too soon to tell. A few days. Maybe up to ten. If that's all…" She scanned the four worried faces. Del spoke for the group.

"That's it for now. Thanks, Doctor."

Offering a tired grin, she dipped her head. "It's my job, Sheriff."

They turned at the sound of boots on the hospital floor. Sarah's mouth went dry at the sight of the woman who'd been with Zane the night before. Lowering her voice, she stepped next to Beth.

"I'm out of here."

"Don't you want to see Zane?"

"I'm not the one he'll want to see." Sarah nodded toward the woman with auburn hair and bright blue eyes.

"That's her?"

"Afraid so. You'll keep me posted?"

"You know I will."

Satisfied, yet regretting the need to leave, Sarah drew away from the group as the woman stopped next to Del.

"Where is he? I want to see him."

"Zane just got out of surgery. They're not letting anyone see him yet." Del introduced Janelle to Kell and Beth. "How about some coffee?"

Holding up a hand, she stared past Del. "Not now."

Other than Beth, no one noticed Sarah's quiet retreat down the hall and out the door.

182

Chapter Twenty-Two

Zane came awake in increments. Eyes opening to slits, he groaned at the pain spreading through his entire body. Licking dry lips, he tried to recall why he was laying in the hospital, feeling as if he'd been the object of a gang beating.

"You're awake." A perky nurse moved beside the bed. "How do you feel?"

He suppressed a sharp reply. "Lousy."

"I'm not surprised."

Trying to raise his left hand, Zane winced. "What's the deal?"

"If you're asking about the status of your injuries, you'll need to speak with the doctor. She should be here soon. On a scale of one to ten, what's your pain level?"

"Five. Maybe a four. Probably good enough to get out of here."

Chuckling, the nurse shook her head as she entered his vitals into Zane's record. "The doctor will determine when you leave."

The door opened as the words left her mouth. "Well, Mr. Talbot. You woke up sooner than I would've suspected. How would you describe your pain level?"

He glanced at the nurse. "Four or lower."

"Uh-huh. We hope to have it lower before you leave. Most of the injuries were minor. Abrasions and contusions. You hit your head pretty hard, so we'll be monitoring you for TBI. The accident caused a tear in your spleen. We completed surgery to remove a portion of it, so you'll need to take it easy so as not to open the sutures. Do you feel you need pain medications right now?"

"No meds. Water would be good."

The nurse picked up the cup holding water, adjusted the straw, and held it against his mouth. Zane finished on a slow nod.

"Over the next few days, you'll be going through a variety of tests. CT scan, blood tests, etc. Your left wrist is sprained, so you'll need to be careful with it." Making a few notes, she looked back at him. "Do you have any questions for me, Mr. Talbot?"

His gaze moved from the doctor to one of the monitors close to her. "How many days will I be here?"

"I'm going to pass on answering that for now. I will say it depends on the results of the tests and how you feel."

His eyes closed. "Fair enough."

"Are you up to having a couple visitors?"

"Hmmm..."

The two women exchanged glances before the doctor spoke. "Let me know when he wakes up again. His family is anxious to see him."

"Yes, Doctor."

Refilling his water cup, the nurse set it aside before adjusting the bed covers. By the time she finished, Zane stirred again, his eyes opening a few seconds later.

"You're still here."

"That I am. If you're up for visitors, I'll let the doctor know. I know there are at least four people in the waiting room. Anyone in particular you want to see?"

"Sarah, if she's out there."

"I'll let the doctor know."

Adjusting his position on the bed, Zane tried to relax. He hoped someone had called Sarah. Would she care he'd been in a crash? He honestly didn't know.

"Who's Sarah?" Janelle crossed her arms and glared at the doctor.

Rather than explaining, Kell changed the subject. "I think Del should go in first. He needs to speak with Zane about the accident."

"Makes no difference to me. Mr. Talbot wanted to see Sarah, and since she isn't here, anyone else?" The doctor looked at Del. "Five minutes maximum. He should be able to spend more time with visitors tomorrow."

"But I should be going in. I'm his fiancée, after all."

Everyone's head turned toward Janelle, their expressions signaling their shock.

"Well, now, that's up to Zane," Kell said. "Afterall, you've been gone a long time, and were with him under less than honest circumstances."

Face flushing, she stomped a foot. "Are you calling me dishonest?"

"What would you call it?"

"All right," Del interrupted. "Let me talk to Zane and we'll go from there. I'll follow you, Doctor."

Beth couldn't hide a smirk at Janelle's reaction. Knowing Zane, that kind of behavior wouldn't go over too well. Then again, she had no idea what Zane's thoughts were regarding her reappearance.

Del followed down the hall before the doctor turned into one of the rooms. "You have a visitor, Mr. Talbot. If you'll both excuse me. And remember, five minutes max."

Eyes opening, Zane felt a twinge of disappointment before recovering. "Hey, Del. Thanks for hanging around."

Grabbing a chair, he dragged it next to the bed. "You won't remember, but I wasn't far behind you when a dually came roaring off a side road and slammed into you."

"You saw it?"

"Both times the truck rammed you. Had a deputy with me, but we weren't able to get the license number. It definitely was a dually, though. I have deputies scouring vehicle records to see if we can identify the owner."

Zane attempted to sit up before falling back down. "I need to get out of here."

"Forget it. You came out of major surgery a few hours ago, and sustained a concussion. What you need is rest, and to do as the doctor orders."

"Yeah, yeah." Zane closed his eyes for a few seconds before opening them to stare out the one large window. "Did anyone call Sarah?"

"Beth contacted her before she and Kell left the house. She came right away, stayed for hours."

"She left?"

"When Janelle showed up and announced she's your fiancée. The statement surprised all of us. Is she?"

Zane's reply was tired yet firm. "No. I don't know what she is, Del. I'd like to see Sarah."

"Not Janelle?"

He didn't immediately reply, preferring to study the various tubes attached to his body. After a while, Zane shook his head.

"Not yet."

"Kell and Beth are in the waiting room. You up for seeing one of them for a few minutes?"

"I need to speak with Kell."

"All right." Del moved to the door. "I'll get him, and figure out something to say to Janelle. You sure you want to see Sarah?"

"If she will come back. I owe her an explanation."

"Maybe give it a day or two. I'll tell Janelle you're too tired to see anyone except Kell right now, and ask Beth to call Sarah."

"Appreciate it." Zane's eyes closed to slits as Del left the room.

Del thought about the accident on his walk through the hospital hallway to the waiting room. Who would want to harm Zane? Who'd want him dead?

Shoving the door open to the waiting area, he spotted Janelle right away. She stood away from Kell and Beth, her features tight. The picture of an angry woman.

Stopping next to where Kell sat, Del bent to whisper close to his ear.

"Zane's tired but wants to speak with you. I'll talk to Janelle."

Rising, Kell cast a quick look at Janelle. "Good luck. She complained for a bit about you going in ahead of her, then planted herself across the room."

Del watched Janelle's expression at Kell entering the hall to Zane's room. Red crept from her neck to her jaw and cheeks. He could almost read what was going through her mind. When she spotted him watching, she turned away. For a minute, he thought she'd grab her bag and leave. Acting before she could, he walked to her.

"Zane's doing fine, but he's very tired. I spoke to him about the accident, and he asked to see Kell. If you don't already know, they're best friends. Zane lives at Beth and Kell's house."

Hands fisted at her sides, she glared at Del. "That doesn't tell me why he doesn't want to see me."

"You must understand that the same as you, he had a life the last ten years."

"Including that Sarah woman?"

"Yes. Zane and Sarah are very close. He's going to rest after Kell leaves. You're welcome to stay. I have to get back to work, but will return later today."

Staring at her feet, she reached toward a nearby chair, grabbing her oversized purse. "I must get to work, too. I'll be back after my shift."

Sarah moved from one task to another without thought. Normally quite social with the patients. Other than cursory greetings, today, she remained silent.

Bathing and grooming one long-time resident, administering medication to another, monitoring vitals for the patients in her wing. All duties were performed by rote. Repetitive tasks she handled five days every week.

Today, all tasks were attacked with a single goal in mind—to keep her thoughts off Zane and his *fiancée.*

"Sarah?"

Stopping her chores of changing the bedding in one room, she straightened to see her supervisor in the doorway. "Yes, Helen?"

"Are you all right?"

"Fine. Why?"

"You seem a little unsettled today."

Shoulders slumping, Sarah sat down on an overstuffed chair in the room. "Zane was run off the road last night. He's in the hospital."

"Why didn't you say something to me earlier? How is he doing?"

"All right, I guess."

"You guess?" Helen sat down at a wooden desk chair.

"I don't know what to think. A woman showed up at the hospital. I left soon after, but Beth told me the woman said she was Zane's fiancée."

"What?" There was a shrillness Sarah seldom heard in Helen's voice.

"She came back to town recently. I saw her and Zane together a few nights ago. It appeared they were just reunited."

"Did you ask Zane about her?"

"No. What would I say? Hey, I saw you kissing another woman. What's going on?"

A grim smile tilted one corner of Helen's mouth. "Sounds good to me."

Sarah snorted a bitter laugh. "I did plan to talk to him. That was before I received the call from Beth telling me he was in the hospital. When the fiancée showed up, I left."

"I see." Pulling a phone from her pocket, Helen made a quick call. "Hello, Jean. It's Helen. Doing fine, thank you. I wonder if you could check something for me. A patient came in last night. Zane Talbot. I don't want information on him, but I know your desk is located at the surgery waiting area. Can you tell me if there's anyone waiting to see him?" She turned toward Sarah. "What does she look like?"

"Average height. Good figure. Strawberry blonde hair."

Helen relayed the information. "Great. I'm sending a friend over who's eager to see him. Her name is Sarah Hutchison. Thanks, Jean. I owe you." Pocketing the phone, she met Sarah's anxious gaze. "The woman isn't there. I want you to time out and head to the hospital. Let Jean know you're there to see Zane. And do not leave if the woman shows up. Until Zane tells you what's going on, don't assume she's anything more than a friend."

Chapter Twenty-Three

Zane's head pounded an excruciating beat, disrupting his ability to recall the events of the night before. He'd eschewed medications to control the pain, wanting to keep his head clear. Pressing fingers to his temples, he wondered if the decision had been a mistake.

Seeing the agony etched on his friend's face, Del closed his notepad. "Why don't I let you rest and come back later?"

"No need." Zane pressed harder. "I've got this."

Sliding the pad into a pocket, he shook his head. "There's no need for you to try and power through this. Might even be better for you to heal a few more days before we go over your recollection of events another time."

"Maybe you're right. I can't seem to concentrate."

"Normal for what you've been through. I'll come back tomorrow. Get some rest, Zane." Del headed for the door, stepping aside to let a lean, though well-muscled, orderly pushing a gurney into the room.

"Thanks. Hey, Mr. Talbot. I'm here to take you to imaging for your MRI appointment."

Del lifted his hand in a brief wave as he left the room. Tugging his phone from a pocket, he waited to place the call until entering the waiting room. Pushing through the doors, his gaze latched onto the lone inhabitant in the room.

"Sarah."

Looking up from the magazine lying ignored in her lap, she set it aside to stand. "Del."

"Did you speak with Beth about visiting?"

"Briefly. She encouraged me to come back, but it was my supervisor who pushed me over the edge by giving me extra time off." She didn't mention Helen's call to the floor nurse. "Did you just come from his room?"

"Yes. They were getting him ready for an MRI. I'm pretty sure they'd let you wait in his room."

"Do you think so?"

Del motioned toward the woman at a desk. "Let's find out. Hello, Jean. This is Sarah Hutchison. She's a good friend of Zane Talbot. Would it be all right if she waited for him in his room?"

Giving Sarah a knowing look, Jean looked at her computer screen before nodding. "He's still at imaging. Could be another twenty minutes."

"That's all right. I don't mind waiting."

"You'll vouch for her, Sheriff?"

"I will."

"All right." Jean gave her the room number. "Just don't stay too long after Mr. Talbot returns."

"I won't. And thank you." Sarah turned to look at Del. "You, too."

"He'll be glad to see you."

"I hope you're right."

Flashing her a thumbs up, he smiled. "I am."

"Here you are, Mr. Talbot. And it looks like you have a visitor." The orderly nodded at Sarah, who stood when they appeared.

She could feel her entire body ripple with anticipation mixed with a strong bit of dread. Forcing herself to relax, she plastered on a smile.

"Sarah?" Transferring to the bed, he continued to watch her.

"Hope it's all right I'm here."

"It's better than all right." Holding out his hand, he relaxed when she threaded her fingers through his. Neither noticed the orderly leaving the room.

"How are you doing?"

"Probably better than I look." Drawing her closer, he kissed the back of her hand.

"You don't look so bad. At least not for a man who rolled down an embankment in his truck. Do they have any idea who did it?"

"Not yet." He studied her face. "You look tired."

One shoulder rose in a shrug. "Maybe a little."

Scooting over, he squeezed her hand. "Sit down."

"There isn't room."

"There's plenty of room, sweetheart."

"Please don't call me that." She hitched herself up on the bed. "Your fiancée isn't going to like it."

"Janelle isn't my fiancée, Sarah."

"Girlfriend, then."

"The last I knew, you were my girlfriend. Did something change?"

When she tried to pull her hand from his, he held on tighter.

"Sarah?"

Staring down at their joined hands, she worked to calm her pounding heart. "Who is she?"

"Ten years ago, she was Debbie Wilson, my fiancée."

"So she didn't die in the accident?"

He let out a long sigh. "Nope."

"How is that possible?"

"It's a long story. I'll tell you all of it once I'm out of here. Right now, I need to rest. Will you stay?"

"As long as they'll let me." Bending down, she pressed her lips to his.

An hour, then two, passed without anyone asking Sarah to leave. Kell came in about seven that evening, surprised yet pleased to see her asleep in one of the two chairs, her hand still gripping Zane's.

Moving his attention to the bed, Kell took an involuntary step backward seeing Zane's eyes wide open and staring at him. Chuckling at himself, he walked to the other side of the bed.

"You look a darned sight better than the last time I was here. How do you feel?"

"Great. Ready to go home."

"I hear ya. Unfortunately, the doctor must approve your leaving. Did you have the MRI?"

Zane cast a look at Sarah. "This afternoon. The tech wouldn't commit to when the doc would have the results. The headache plaguing me finally disappeared a couple hours ago."

"About the time Sarah arrived?"

A smile brightened Zane's features. "Just about. How is everything at the ranch?"

"Busy. Construction of the second barn is going well. Everything at the stables is fine. Rona Kessler asked about you. I didn't mention the accident. She mentioned Janelle. Told me they've been friends since they were kids in Texas."

Zane's eyes widened at the news. "Then she must know Janelle and I were together in high school."

"I thought the same. I'll wager Janelle doesn't know Rona has been stalking you."

"Not exactly stalking. Nothing I couldn't handle."

Kell rubbed the back of his neck. "I don't think Rona knew anything about WITSEC. She told me they hadn't been in touch since they were fourteen. The two were reunited in Whiskey Bend. There's a chance she didn't know about your history with Janelle."

"Benefit of the doubt? Yeah, I can live with that. Any sign of Janelle in the waiting area?"

"I expected to see her when I got off the elevator. She wasn't anywhere around. Doesn't mean she isn't out there now. You'll need to tell her about Sarah sometime."

Zane didn't have time to respond. Sarah yawned, stretching out the legs curled under her. Glancing at the two men, she gave an apologetic grin.

"Did I miss the party?"

Zane tugged her out of the chair. "You didn't miss a thing. Kell just got here. He was giving me an update on work at the ranch."

"Speaking of the ranch, I'd best be getting back. I'll be back tomorrow." Kell moved to the door, then whirled around. "Beth's been trying to reach you, Sarah." He closed the door behind him.

She pulled out her phone, seeing three missed calls. She read the text from Beth, brows drawing together, causing deep creases between her eyes.

"Bad news?"

Lifting her head to look at Zane, she shook her head. "I'm not sure. Beth's text says someone left two envelopes by the front door. One for me and one for you. She didn't open them. Probably nothing."

Checking voicemail, one from Beth said the same as her text. The other two were from her supervisor, Helen.

"Should I pick up the envelopes from Beth and bring them back here?"

"No. You don't need to be my delivery service."

"I'm not. When are visiting hours over?"

"Nine, I think."

"Plenty of time." She brushed her lips across his. "I'll be back soon."

Zane watched her leave, feeling an odd sense of loss. He hadn't planned to get in so deep with Sarah. Best laid plans and all that.

Staring at the ceiling, he considered the time since first taking her out. Their relationship was easy, requiring little work. Sarah didn't do drama or make demands. She had a great sense of humor, and unlike him, she never met a stranger.

Her goal of a teaching degree kept her focused. Whatever the reason, they just seemed to fit.

His thoughts moved to Janelle. Their relationship had never been easy. She'd tended to react to everything from a tiny stain on a blouse to being knocked aside in the high school hallway. All were a ten on the Richter scale. Funny how he'd never noticed until now.

They'd fought a lot in high school, mostly for silly reasons. The same reasons both forgot fifteen minutes later. Janelle held herself aloof, making few friends. Much of her behavior became clear now that he knew about her life in WITSEC.

Two issues gnawed at him. Janelle had grown accustomed to moving as it pleased her. A year in Oregon, the next in Wyoming, the following in New Mexico. She'd pack her bags and take off on a whim. The lifestyle she preferred didn't interest him.

The other issue bothered Zane the most. Her parents had been dead for at least three years. If his guess was correct, she hadn't even considered trying to find him.

Janelle had continued with her wanderlust, visiting places as it suited her.

If he'd been in her situation, he would've done everything possible to find her. Janelle's desires had been different. Where Sarah focused on others, Janelle's actions were targeted inward. His mother had once told him some people were givers while others were takers. Labeling the two women wasn't difficult.

Something else niggled at the edges of his consciousness. He hadn't missed Janelle since the night they were reunited. The thrill of seeing her again hadn't solidified the old emotions of deep love. It was different with Sarah.

Zane already missed her, and she'd left a scant fifteen minutes earlier. He thought of her before falling asleep, and immediately upon waking. Working at the ranch, he forced himself not to call her several times a day, replacing the urges with a few text messages.

Right now, he wanted to call her, make certain she'd arrived at the ranch without incident. All his protective instincts centered on Sarah.

Zane understood the emotion squeezing his chest while thickening his throat until it was hard to swallow. He never imagined it would happen twice. Unprepared for what would come next, he reminded himself the emotion he felt had a name.

Love.

Chapter Twenty-Four

Janelle reread the note she'd received in a plain white envelope for the fourth time. Nothing changed with each reading. Fear gripped her, making it hard to breathe.

Though it was eight at night, she'd called her U.S Marshall protector after the second read. Any minute, he'd ring the doorbell and walk into her tiny, studio apartment. Once he had a chance to study the note, they'd discuss strategies and tactics to counter the threat.

A hard knock preceded Tom Dekker's entry. He walked toward her, holding out a hand already covered in a latex glove. Perusing it quickly, his features hardened. The threats were plain, the assailant implied.

"We're right back where we started, Tom." Janelle wanted to cry, but showing weakness wasn't allowed. "Even without proof, you know it's the Maldonado Cartel." She started to pace around the tiny space, balling junk mail into balls, tossing them in all directions. "What do they want from me? I know nothing about what my father saw. Isn't that what the trial was about? The two oldest Maldonado brothers were found guilty, and are in prison for years. Even if I knew something, I'd never refute my father's testimony."

Tom got as close to her as he felt comfortable. She had a temper, which he'd been the recipient of many times over the years.

"They're sending a message. Not just to us, but to anyone who may consider testifying against the cartel."

She snorted. "This is what will happen if you go against us?"

"Exactly. They want to make an example of you. Not only will they go after those who actually testify. The cartel will go after family members, including women and children. Trust me, their method has been used for centuries, and is quite effective."

Dropping into a chair, she buried her face in her hands. "I don't want to move again. My job is great, my apartment is affordable, and I like the town."

"And Zane Talbot is here."

"I need to see him, Tom." That's when a light went off in her head. "Do you think the cartel ran him off the road?"

"Yes." He sat across from her, crossing his legs.

"That's it? Yes?"

"What more is there to say? We knew this could happen if you developed friendships. Zane's an old friend. Therefore, he's the perfect target. Killing him would cause you pain, and send you a message."

"None of this makes sense." Swiping away an angry tear, she shoved up from the chair, looked around, then sat down again.

"Doesn't have to. What you have to do is everything it takes to stay alive."

A slow shake of her head, more swiping of tears, then she seemed to mentally collapse within herself. Eyes closed, she continued to leak a slow stream of tears.

Tom rose and headed to the kitchen. He returned a few minutes later with a hot cup of chamomile tea. Touching her shoulder, he held out the cup.

"Drink this, Janelle. Then we have to get moving."

Opening her eyes, she took the cup. "I'm not moving again." Blowing across the top, she swallowed a few sips before cradling the cup in both hands.

"If you want to live, we have to leave Whiskey Bend."

"And go where? We've moved all over since I was fourteen. The cartel always finds me. Relocating won't solve the basic problem that there's no place where I'll be safe."

Lowering himself onto the sofa, his features softened. "There is one place we can go where no one will ever find you."

She waited for a long minute, wondering if he was going to tell her the location this magical place was, where one of the largest and most ruthless cartels couldn't find her. When he cleared his throat, she prepared herself for an answer she wouldn't necessarily like.

"There's this cabin. Well, more than a standard cabin. It's on a lake, with five bedrooms, six baths, modern kitchen, huge great room with a river rock fireplace. It's off the grid, in the sense the property is titled in the name of a corporation, which is buried within other corporations."

A slow smile began brightening her face. "Sounds very black ops."

"In a sense, it is." Standing, he walked while rubbing the back of his neck. "The place seems to be a hundred miles from civilization, yet it's about ten minutes from a quaint mountain town with a gas station, grocery, department store, beauty salon. It's also an hour from a larger town, with anything you'd want."

"Sounds wonderful. Why haven't we gone there before?"

He stopped pacing to give her a significant look. "There's always been a barrier to using it. That barrier no longer exists."

Turning his back to her, he rummaged in the refrigerator, taking out a beer. "You want anything besides the tea?"

"No, thanks. I'm waiting for the punch line."

Chuckling, he opened the can and took a long draw. He remained silent until he joined her back in the combination living room/bedroom. Sitting, he took another swallow of his beer.

"It must be pretty bad if it's this hard to give me the rest of the details."

"Not bad at all. I'm still trying to adjust to a few changes."

Her brows drew together. "Changes?"

"You already know both my grandfather and father were U.S. Senators."

"Yeah, I remember. You come from a wealthy family, and were ostracized for not following them into politics."

"Good memory. What you don't know is my father died of cancer several months ago."

"Oh, Tom. I'm so sorry. Why didn't you say anything?"

"No reason to. I didn't plan to attend the services. No one to visit. Mother died years ago, and I have no brothers or sisters. It was almost a non-event."

She waited, knowing there was more.

"Anyway, turns out he kept me in his will. Everything came to me, including the house on the lake."

"You own the house?"

"Yes."

"You want me to live in your house?"

"It is the safest place I know. Nothing would change from other places you've been. The fact I'm the owner makes no real difference. The ownership is still buried in an almost impossible maze of corporations. You'd have to give up any friendships you've made in Whiskey Bend. Again, nothing you haven't done before."

"Except I'd give up what I considered a new life here."

"Yes. You'd have to walk away from your job...and from Zane."

Janelle thought of the man she'd loved for so long. There'd been other boyfriends, none had compared to Zane. She'd thought freedom had finally been granted to her and they'd have another chance.

Of course, she would've had to convince him to join her nomadic lifestyle. She'd grown accustomed to new adventures in various locations. Her plan had been to keep Whiskey Bend as a home base, spending a few months a year somewhere else. She'd been certain Zane could've been talked into joining her. Now?

"It's about making a choice, Janelle. Your life versus what could be a few short weeks or months with Zane. But you must have a decision now. If it's to leave, we have to get out of here tonight."

Jumping up, hands fisted at her sides, she shook her head. "I need more time."

"You don't have that luxury. If you don't believe me, read the note again. My gear is already packed. We'll leave your car—"

"No!" She glanced around the tiny studio apartment. Nothing but a few sticks of furniture and walls. One big box with no personality and little warmth. The first place she'd paid for with her own money.

Her job at the feed store was what she'd chosen, not what Tom had lined up for her. She'd selected and paid for the car, and he wanted her to leave it. Walk away from her own meager achievements.

Her life or Zane. An impossible choice.

"You know he's in love with Sarah Hutchison."

Her head whipped toward Tom, pain flashing in her features.

"I'm sorry, Janelle, but you have to accept the truth. If he still cared, you would've been the one he asked for at the hospital. Instead, it's been Sarah who's visited him." He walked to her, placing hands on her shoulders. "I don't say this to hurt you. You'll have a real life at the lake house."

"I still won't be able to use my own name."

"No, you won't."

"What would I do there?"

"Whatever you want. We'll change you to a platinum blonde, or perhaps a redhead."

"You've always said red is too conspicuous."

Eyes crinkling at the corners, he smiled, sensing victory. "It is."

"I'll think about it."

"You don't have to decide about your hair tonight."

Sucking in a slow breath, when she spoke, her voice sounded resigned. "I know."

He walked to the small closet, tugging out two duffels. Placing them on the sofa, he shoved both hands into pockets. "You need to pack."

She didn't answer, the usual wariness in her expression replaced by a sadness Tom had witnessed often in the years he'd been her protector, counselor, and occasional best friend.

"I need to give Willow two week's notice."

"You aren't able to do that."

"She'll be a bad reference if I don't give her time to replace me." Using the zipper, she took her time opening one duffel.

"Willow will never be contacted. References will happen in the usual way."

A brow rose. "Through the Marshal's Service?"

"The notes will work to our favor with my supervisor. We won't need their help with a place to live. This request will be easy for them."

"What if they decide to replace you?"

"That won't happen, Janelle. After this long, there isn't a remote chance they'll send someone else in." Walking to the dresser, he opened the top drawer. "Let's get you packed."

"Not yet."

"Why not?"

"There's something I have to do first."

Crossing his arms, he released a tired sigh. "What?" He was afraid he already knew the answer.

She ran a hand along the back of a nearby chair. Tom wouldn't like her answer, but it wasn't his decision to make.

"I want to talk to Zane."

Chapter Twenty-Five

Sheriff Del Macklin slammed a hand onto his desk, frustrated at the lack of progress on locating the dually who'd run Zane off the road. At seven in the morning, he'd hoped there would be some good news. There were several dozen of the large trucks in the county, mostly owned by ranchers.

Some had been driven out of town before the incident, others were no longer working. The remaining trucks showed no signs of being in a recent accident. His deputies had checked each one, putting in long hours driving all over the county. Most of the ranchers had cooperated, others had complained, making the chore more difficult. Bottom line, all the work had been for nothing.

Without a physical description of the driver, and no residual paint on Zane's truck, the investigation came to a halt. Del couldn't have been more frustrated.

Not once had he considered calling U.S. Marshal Tom Dekker. Why would he? The man hadn't been on the scene.

"There's a man here to see you, Sheriff."

Del glanced up from the open file. "Who?"

"Tom Dekker. He's a U.S. Marshal. Want me to send him back?"

"I'll go out. Thanks." Following his deputy to the front, he held out a hand. "Hey, Tom. What brings you in here?"

"Do you have a few minutes to talk?"

"Sure. We'll go to my office. Would you like some coffee?"

"No, thanks. This won't take long."

Closing the door behind them, Del motioned to a chair. "How can I help you?"

"I may have some information for you."

"Regarding what?"

"The people who ran Zane Talbot off the road."

"I'd appreciate whatever information you have."

Tom took several minutes telling Del about the Maldonado Cartel and his theory on their connection to the incident.

"It's just my take on it, Sheriff. Take it for what it is." Standing, he headed to the door.

"How's Janelle doing?"

The question surprised Tom. "All right. Why?"

"No real reason. She hasn't shown up to visit Zane since the night of the crash."

"I think she realizes her time with Zane has passed. He seems pretty connected to Sarah Hutchison. She's not going to try to break that up."

"How'd she learn about Sarah?"

Shrugging, Tom rested his hand on the doorknob. "It's my job to check out everyone who comes in contact with Janelle. I learned about Sarah and did some research. Wasn't hard to learn how tight she and Zane are."

Del nodded in understanding. "Will she be staying in Whiskey Bend?"

"Does it matter?"

"Guess not. It's a good place to live. I know Willow is pleased with her work."

"If the cartel has found her..." Tom didn't finish, letting Del come to his own conclusion.

A moment passed before he gave a nod. "Understood."

"I need to head out. Thanks for your time, Sheriff."

"Appreciate it, Tom. Take care of yourself."

He touched his forehead in a mock salute. "Will do."

Janelle's steps were almost silent as she walked down the hall to Zane's room. She wanted to be the first in and out during visiting hours. Pushing the door open, her heart skipped at the sight of Zane wide awake and sitting up. His gaze locked on her. Nothing in his expression gave away his thoughts.

"Good morning, Zane."

"Janelle."

"I hope it's all right for me to be here."

"Of course it is. I'm surprised you haven't been here before now. Pull up a chair."

Dragging a chair closer to the bed, she sat down. "You look better than I'd imagined. How do you feel?"

"Much better. I'm hoping to get out of here later today."

"I'll bet you're anxious to get back to work."

"I am." His gaze wandered over her, seeing a completely different woman than the one he'd met in the feed store parking lot. "Are you all right?"

Clasping her hands together, she looked away as her back went rigid. She'd practiced her speech over and over. Sitting in his room, she couldn't recall a word.

"Janelle."

"I, uh…thought this would be easier."

"Talk to me. Explain what's going on."

Unable to stay seated, she stood, walking to the window. Placing a hand on the glass, she bowed her head as if in prayer.

"You know about me being in WITSEC. What you don't know is the Maldonado Cartel is still after me."

He sat up straighter. "Why? Did you witness their actions?"

"Not at all. It's so frustrating because there's nothing I can tell them. I certainly can't get their men out of prison."

"What does Tom think?"

She moved toward the bed. "He believes they're sending a message."

"Testify against the cartel and there will be consequences."

"Exactly. Tom also believes it was the cartel who ran you off the road."

Zane's eyes widened, though he said nothing.

"I'm so sorry I brought this danger to you. If I'd known, I never would've come to Whiskey Bend."

"Come here." He held out his hand. Closing the distance between them, she took it. "Their actions aren't your fault. For the record, I'm glad you came here."

"You are?"

"Of course. All these years, I thought you'd died in the accident. Learning you're alive means a great deal to me, Janelle."

"Even if the accident was staged?"

"Not that I understand the reasons behind your actions, yes. What I haven't been able to figure out is why you stayed away so long after the trial and the deaths of your parents. Why didn't you come to me then?"

Unable to meet his questioning gaze, she stared at their joined hands. "I don't have a good answer for you. Fear, maybe."

"About what?"

She raised one shoulder in a shrug. "Fear you wouldn't understand why I had to leave. That you'd hate me."

"I could never hate you."

She pulled her hand from his. "But you don't love me anymore, do you?"

Zane looked away. He knew the answer, yet wasn't prepared to discuss his feelings for her or Sarah.

"You're going to have to answer the question sometime. Now would be good."

Heart pounding, he lifted his gaze to hers. "No, I don't love you anymore."

She fought the urge to cry. Somewhere inside, a part of her wanted him to admit he did love her. It wasn't to be. And that was for the best. With the cartel after her, she had no desire to put him, or anyone else, in danger.

She bit her lip, determined not to shed tears over his admission. "I'm leaving Whiskey Bend and won't be back."

"Why?"

Forcing a grin, she tried for levity. "It's what I do, Zane. Run when the cartel gets too close."

"Don't go, Janelle. We'll pull strings. Get extra protection for you."

"I appreciate the thought, but it's for the best. Besides, there's this fabulous cabin on a lake waiting for me."

What she would never tell him was there wasn't a chance she'd be able to watch Zane build a life with Sarah. Janelle may have been wrong to stay away, but she did still love him.

"Are you sure?"

"Absolutely. Besides, I'm a wanderer. Even without the cartel after me, it would only be a matter of time before I'd leave for a new adventure." Stepping closer, she ran a finger down his cheek. "You are the best man I've ever known. I wish..." She couldn't finish. Instead, she pressed a kiss to his lips. Lifting her head, she stared into beautiful eyes for what she knew would be the last time. "I will always love you."

Before she broke down, Janelle ran from the room, ignoring his shouts not to leave.

Zane rolled out of his own bed four days later, still tired from a restless night. He'd been cleared to leave the hospital the same day Janelle had disappeared.

She'd ghosted, as if never living in Whiskey Bend. He hadn't expected to feel such despair at her disappearance. Her leaving gave him freedom to pursue Sarah without worrying about hurting Janelle. Then why had he only spoken to Sarah once since returning home?

Zane knew his feelings for her were real. He loved Sarah, wanted to build a life with her, including as many children as she'd be willing to give him.

He'd called her once, discouraging her from coming to the house. The excuse of requiring a little time to get caught up with his work didn't go over well, yet she'd accepted it and stayed away.

Beth hadn't been happy with him, poking at Zane to invite Sarah over. He knew Beth was right, and promised to call her.

Today, he would.

Dressing, he headed downstairs, following the aroma of coffee. The kitchen was empty. He knew Beth would've already left for her job at the law firm, and Kell would be out with the horses or working on the second barn.

A note on the table told him Beth had left breakfast warming in the oven. Opening the door, he used a potholder to remove a plate heaped with bacon and pancakes. His stomach growled.

"Thank you, Beth," he muttered to himself, chewing a piece of bacon.

He ate every bite, the pancakes spread with butter and smothered in the best syrup he'd ever tasted. When finished, he rinsed the plate and utensils, setting them in the dishwasher.

Eight o'clock. Sarah would be almost on the road to work. Drawing his phone from a pocket, he hit her speed dial. The call went to voicemail.

"Sarah, it's Zane. Do you have time for dinner this week? Any day is good for me. Let me know what works and I'll pick you up. Talk to you soon."

Ending the call, he pocketed the phone, anxious to hear back.

Three days passed without her returning his call.

Chapter Twenty-Six

Sarah stared at another message from Zane, unable to summon up the energy to read it. His refusal to call her after returning from the hospital had hurt. Without confirmation from him, she'd decided he'd decided to try to make it work with Janelle. That hurt even more.

Even after Beth assured her Janelle was no longer in Zane's life, Sarah hesitated returning his calls. Perhaps her cousin was right and he needed a little time to heal completely while returning to work. So be it. She wanted a little downtime, too, and tonight, Sarah would be meeting an old friend at Wicked Waters.

Friday night, and the place was hopping. Sarah stood inside, scanning the tables for Brock Pattin. They'd dated briefly a couple years earlier, before he took a job out of state. Never more than friends, they continued to exchange text messages and the occasional phone call.

"Sarah!"

She shifted her attention to a man to her right. Brock waved a hand in the air. Waving back, she slipped between tables to join him.

"You look gorgeous, as always." He wrapped her in his arms, placing a kiss on her forehead.

"You look pretty great yourself." And he did. Brock was the cliché of tall, dark, and handsome. Even in the past, when they'd come into Wicked Waters together, the flow of women to their table had been nonstop. She expected nothing less tonight.

"What do you want to drink?"

She looked at his beer. "What are you having?"

"Bitterroot Brewery IPA."

"I'll have the same."

Waving down a waitress, he ordered. "How are you, princess?"

She laughed at the nickname he'd given her not long after they'd met. "Good. Better than good, really. Work and school are going well. How about you?"

"The same. I've saved enough for a down payment on a ranch in northern Wyoming. I've already spoken with the current owner, and he's willing to discuss terms."

"That's wonderful, Brock. I know you've been saving for years."

"Thanks, Sarah. It's not a large spread, but plenty for my purposes. I'd love to have you come down and see it."

"I'd love to see it."

The waitress arrived with her beer and a bowl of pretzels.

When Sarah went for her purse, Brock waved her off. "It's on my tab." Lifting his beer, he held it out to her. "To you coming to see my ranch."

Touching her glass to his, she took a long swallow. "I love this song. Let's dance."

"Whatever you want, princess." Taking her hand, he led her to the dance floor.

They two-stepped along with the other couples, then moved into a Cowboy Cha-Cha when the song changed. He tucked her close on the third song, an older ballad by George Strait.

"I don't know why we never got together, princess."

She smiled into his shoulder. "Because we're much better friends, and we didn't want to ruin it."

"Did I agree to that?"

"You suggested it, Brock."

"That may have been the dumbest thing I've ever said." He ran a hand down her hair, pressing a kiss to her head. "Can we revisit it?"

Smiling, she squeezed his hand. "Maybe someday. So, whose spell have you fallen under?"

"I don't know what you mean."

"What starstruck young woman is waiting for you back in Wyoming?"

"Not a one, princess. I'm all yours." When the song ended, he escorted her back to their table. Pulling out her chair, he noticed a tall cowboy walking toward them, his gaze locked on Sarah.

Ignoring Brock, he stopped in front of her. "Good evening, sweetheart."

Sarah's head whipped upward, eyes going wide. Her heart flipped. "Hello, Zane."

He held out his hand to the other man. "Zane Talbot."

Grasping the outstretched hand, Brock gave a terse nod. "Brock Pattin. You a friend of Sarah's?"

"Well, now, that's a real good question. Sarah? Am I your friend?"

Swallowing, she nodded. "Yes, you are."

"Am I still your boyfriend?"

Brock hid a grin.

"Well…"

"It's a simple question, sweetheart."

"Yes, I believe you are."

Brock smiled at her demure manner. Something he'd never witnessed in Sarah. "Excellent. You'll have to join us, Zane. Have you ordered yet?"

"Not yet."

"Great. What can I get you?"

Zane glanced at Brock's glass. "Whatever you're drinking is fine."

"Great. I'll be right back, kids. Play nice while I'm gone."

Turning toward Sarah, he rested his arms on the table. "What's going on, Sarah?"

She didn't answer right away, preferring to watch the couples on the dance floor. Not that she had an answer for him. Meeting Brock had been spur of the moment. Brock was in town a few days and wanted to get together. As a friend, of course she'd say yes.

"Brock and I are friends, Zane. Have been for a few years. He's in town, and we met here. Nothing more to it."

He took in her brief explanation of tonight, not touching on why she hadn't returned his calls. "I've left messages for you."

"I know. It was a busy week with work and classes."

Brock arrived with a beer for each of them. "There's a line out front to get in. Never saw that before."

"Josh Reyes spoke to Kull. Guess it's been happening more often." Zane took a sip of his beer, then looked at Sarah before his gaze swung to the front door. "Kull hired front door security for Fridays and Saturdays. A new employee at Josh's shop."

"He owns the custom motorcycle shop, right?" Brock watched the dance floor as he gulped down part of his beer.

"Thorn Macklin, Josh, and Tony Coletti own it. They have business coming in from all over the western U.S." Zane looked between Brock and Sarah, wondering if their friendship crossed over into more.

"Another dance, Sarah?" Brock set down his beer.

"Sure."

Zane watched them make their way between tables to the already crowded dance floor. Two-stepping had given way to individual moves while facing their partner. The dance which had been around for decades. The number of people forced people to dance closer to each other than usual, Brock and Sarah were no more than six to eight inches apart.

"Hey, stranger."

Zane shifted to see Faith beside him. "Evening, Faith. How are you?"

"Good. I heard you were the driver of the truck that was run off the road. You doing okay?"

“I am now.”

“Feeling good enough to dance?”

Hesitating for an instant, he stood. “Sure.”

Taking her hand, he navigated the tables to find an opening within several feet of Brock and Sarah on the dance floor. The fast country beat gave way to a slow song. Faith moved into his arms. She fit him. Maybe better than Sarah, but it didn’t feel right.

He glanced to where Sarah danced with Brock. Her gaze locked with Zane’s. A silent message seemed to pass between them.

When the song ended, he escorted Faith to where her friends sat. “Thank you.”

“Maybe we can dance another later.” Her voice was tinged with hope.

“Perhaps.” He bent, kissed her forehead, shifted to return to his table, and almost ran into Sarah. Features blank, she didn’t look pleased or angry at him dancing with Faith.

“Would you dance with me, Zane?”

“Anytime, Sarah.”

She threaded her fingers through his as they walked to the dance floor. Walking into his arms, they moved to the beat of a slow dance. Zane felt as if he’d come home.

"Janelle's gone, Zane. Tom Dekker helped pack her few belongings, and they left Whiskey Bend the same day she visited you at the hospital." Del sat atop his horse, the two watching a small herd of cattle.

It had been three weeks since he'd been released from the hospital. He'd spent some of his free time making last minute adjustments to his computer app, and the rest with Sarah. He hadn't tried to reach Janelle, nor did he ask Willow if she was still working at the feed store.

"Did Dekker leave you any information on how to contact her?"

"None, which is to be expected. He treats this as if she were still in WITSEC. Why do you want to talk to her?"

Zane removed his hat, threading fingers through his hair before settling it back down. "She said a few things at the hospital which surprised me. I didn't have a response then."

"You do now?"

Watching a group of three steers move around each other, he thought of what he'd say to Janelle. "I do."

"Will it change anything between you and Janelle, or you and Sarah?"

"Not really." Zane had held onto his love for Janelle so long, he found it hard to put her in his past.

"Are you in love with Sarah?"

"Yes."

"Then let it go, Zane. No good will come your way by trying to track down Janelle."

His friend was right. A life with Sarah loomed in his future. Jeopardizing it would be short-sighted and foolish.

"Janelle isn't her legal name."

Zane's head whipped toward Del. "But..."

"Tom dropped that on me before he left my office. She hasn't used her real name since she was fourteen. Dekker doubts she'll ever use it again."

The sound of an approaching horse drew their attention. Kell reined up beside Zane. "You two ready to move these bad boys to another pasture?"

"Whenever you are." Del reined his horse around, but not before seeing the stunned expression on Zane's face.

Kell saw it, too. "You all right?"

"Yeah. Let's get this done."

Holding two bags of takeout, Zane stood outside Sarah's house. When she didn't answer his knock, he pulled out the key she'd given him.

It had been a surprise to feel her tuck it into his hand after dinner a few nights earlier. They'd cooked at her place, Zane seasoning and barbequing the steaks while she prepared vegetables and a salad. The meal had been excellent, so had the conversation, including a decision to go for another ride over the weekend.

They hadn't been together long. In Zane's mind, it had been long enough for him to know he wanted to spend his life with Sarah. The house key had been her way of telling him she agreed.

Setting the food on the kitchen counter, he pulled out plates, utensils, and napkins. He expected Sarah soon, as she had less than ninety minutes to eat and get to class. If work at the ranch finished early tomorrow, he'd cook. Maybe his famous chicken enchiladas with guacamole.

Sarah pushed the front door open and stepped inside. "Smells great in here."

Zane looked up from where he was transferring food into serving bowls. "Hey."

He walked to her, taking her into his arms, and kissing her soundly. The contact took on a life of its own until they ended up on the sofa in an embrace neither seemed eager to break.

Coming up for air, Zane slid hair from her face before placing a final kiss on her forehead. "That's a welcome I could get used to."

Eyes glassy with passion, Sarah chuckled. "Same here."

Zane pressed a kiss to her temple. "Guess we should eat."

"Guess so."

Throwing back his head, he laughed at the disappointment in her voice. Standing, he leaned down, picking her up, then setting her on her feet.

Reaching up, she brushed a kiss across his lips before walking to the short hallway. "I'll wash my hands and be back to help you."

Zane had their food on the table and glasses of water for each of them on the table by the time she returned. "There's plenty, so plan to eat a lot, sweetheart."

She stared at the choices, smiling up at him. "You went to the new Korean barbeque."

"You've been talking about going, and I decided it was time we tried them." Pulling out a chair, he seated her, then took the chair beside her. "I bought a little of everything."

"Smells wonderful."

Filling their plates, they talked and ate for almost an hour, until Sarah had to leave for class.

"I'll call you tomorrow." He planted a kiss on her lips before she slipped out the front door. Filling the dishwasher, he looked around. It was a great little house. He knew Thorn and Grace owned it, and were glad to rent it to Sarah.

If they married, where would they live?

The question punched him in the gut. He'd thought of marriage in the abstract, never going into the reality of asking her. Did he love her enough to spend the rest of his life with her? He knew the answer.

Sarah dismounted and ground tied her horse before running to the edge of the trail to look down. A hundred yards below, fast moving Whiskey Creek pounded through the base of the valley.

"This is fantastic, Zane. Have you been here before?"

He stopped behind her, placing his hands on her waist. "A couple times with Kell. The locals call it Murphy's Drop."

"Why?"

"Because some guy named Murphy came up here roaring drunk and dropped off the cliff."

She looked over her shoulder at him. "That's horrible."

"But true." He tugged her against him, wrapping his arms around her.

"I'll bet there are a lot of places up here worth seeing. Doesn't seem as if it's heavily traveled."

"Hard to tell. The easiest way to reach the trail is from our ranch. If you ride from the public trailhead, it takes almost two hours to get to the turnoff, which winds up here. The entire round trip is at least six hours. Long for a day trip."

She rested her hands on his. "Then us being here is even more special."

Kissing her neck, he rested his chin on the top of her head. "I'm glad you like it."

"I love it."

Lowering his voice, Zane whispered next to her ear. "I love you, Sarah."

Stilling in his arms, she slowly turned to look up at him. "What?"

"I know it may be too soon, but I've fallen in love with you."

Slipping her hands up his arms and around his neck, she stared into gorgeous blue eyes. "I love you, too, Zane."

The roaring creek below served as the ideal backdrop for the kiss that followed. He held her close, stroking his hands over and down her back to rest on the swell of her hips.

Lifting his head, Zane rested his forehead against hers. He'd never felt this connected to any woman. Not even Janelle…or whatever her name was.

Stepping back, he took her hands in his. "I have this crazy notion, Sarah."

"Are you going to share it?"

A nervous smile flitted across his face. "Marry me."

She stood in stunned silence for a minute before breaking into laughter. "Is that a proposal?"

Undeterred, he grinned along with her. "It is. Short and to the point. What do you say?"

The laughter dissolving, she looked down at their joined hands. "I do love you, Zane. Very much." Glancing up, tears burning behind her eyes, she gave an almost imperceptible nod. "Yes, I'll marry you."

"For better or for worse?"

"For better or for worse."

Epilogue

One month later...

"Tyler Macklin. Get your dogs out of the kitchen." Willow crossed her arms, glaring at her and Boone's son run through the house to catch the youngest of his two dogs. "One, two..."

"I've got him, Mom." Tyler held his collar, tugging the hundred pound dog through the kitchen and outside. At nine, the dog weighed more than him. "I'll put him in one of the stalls."

Willow shook her head, looking at a very pregnant Amy for support. "I don't know what possessed me to offer our house for the wedding."

"Because you're a nice person and knew Beth's place wasn't big enough to accommodate everyone." Amy reached for a chair, plopping onto the seat a little harder than intended. "I will be so glad when the baby comes."

"You're due anytime, right?"

"Yes. I'm just praying he doesn't come tomorrow during the wedding. The reception is fine, but not the ceremony." Arching, she pressed a hand against the small of her back. "The doctor estimates he's going to be over nine pounds."

Willow hid her surprise. "You'll be able to handle it, whatever his weight."

"That's what Del says. I hope you're both right."

"Hello."

"We're in the kitchen, Sarah."

Joining them, she set a large cardboard box on the table. "A few items for the wedding. Beth thought it would be better if I brought them over today." She hugged Amy, then Willow. "Thanks again for volunteering your home. Zane and I aren't taking a honeymoon right now, so I'll be back on Sunday to help clean up."

"You will not." Willow's voice allowed no argument. "I already have people lined up to do the cleanup. Even if you're not going anywhere, you and Zane deserve a day all to yourselves."

"Are you sure, because I don't mind coming over."

"Absolutely. What I do need help with is setting up the tables and chairs outside. Boone and Thorn already set up the canopies."

Bending forward to stretch her back, Amy looked out a window to the front yard. "How many people are you expecting, Willow?"

"Twenty, plus or minus. The Macklins, Kell and Beth, Josh and Tony and their plus ones, Kull, and a few others. Not too many at all." Willow opened the refrigerator doors, showing already prepared food. "Some of this needs to be warmed up, but most goes from here to the serving tables. Josh and Tony will take care of barbequing."

Closing the doors, Willow smiled at Sarah. "All you and Zane have to do is show up."

"I now pronounce you man and wife. Zane, you may kiss your bride."

Zane dipped Sarah, kissing her deeply before raising his head and setting her back on her feet. The whistles, shouts, and cheers sounded like more than twenty-two people.

The people witnessing the ceremony didn't part when Zane and Sarah walked toward them. Instead, they enveloped the couple, hugging her and clasping his back before breaking into small groups.

Josh stood next to Detective Maggie O'Dell. Her eight-year-old daughter, Ashley, had long ago abandoned her mother to play with Tyler. Maggie, on call for her job, held a soda, while Josh nursed a beer. It had become common to see them together around town, even though everyone knew there was no romantic involvement.

"Hey, Josh." Tony clasped his good friend on the shoulder. "You ready to fire up the barbeque?"

"Whenever you are."

"Then let's get this party going." Placing an arm over the shoulders of his date, Tony kissed her cheek. "Are you all right hanging with Maggie for a while, Jillian?"

"Of course. Go make delicious food." When the men were out of earshot, she turned toward Maggie.

Across the open space, Del stood next to Boone, their attention on Josh. "Do you ever think Josh and Maggie will figure out they're meant to be together?" Del sipped a beer, tipping it toward their friend.

"Not unless Josh falls on his head and gets some sense knocked into him. The guy's as stubborn as they come, and Maggie's no better. She's determined no man will ever be able to replace her deceased husband. Anyway, none of my business. I'm going to see if Willow needs any help." Boone got to within a few feet of the steps when a gasp came from his left.

Amy was bent at the waist, staring at the ground. Willow stood beside her, a comforting hand on her friend's back.

"What is it?" It was then Boone noticed the dampness at Amy's feet.

"Her water broke. Go get Del."

Boone was already moving.

Amy let out a low groan. "This is exactly what I didn't want to happen."

"Well, it did. Let's get you inside and cleaned up." Wrapping an arm around Amy's waist, she helped her to the bathroom. "I have a couple things you can use. I'll be right back."

Willow got a few feet away when Amy let out a loud scream. "Don't go, Willow. Get Del. I think the baby is coming."

Boots pounding on the wood floor came toward them. "Amy?"

"In the bathroom. Hurry."

Opening the door, Del found his wife on the floor, her knees drawn up, her face flushed and damp.

"Call 9-1-1."

They didn't have time. With the combined efforts of guests with medical training, including Zane, Bryce Delaware Macklin entered the world thirty minutes later.

Learn about upcoming books in the Macklins of Whiskey Bend series at https://geni.us/MaklinsofWhiskeBendSer

Enjoy the Macklin brothers? Here's another series you might want to read. MacLarens of Fire Mountain Contemporary Western Romance series.

If you want to keep current on all my preorders, new releases, and other happenings, sign up for my newsletter at: http://www.shirleendavies.com/contact-me.html

A Note from Shirleen

233

Thank you for taking the time to read **Zane**!

If you enjoyed it, please consider telling your friends or posting a short review. Word of mouth is an author's best friend and much appreciated.

I care about quality, so if you find something in error, please contact me via email at
shirleen@shirleendavies.com

Books by Shirleen Davies

Contemporary Western Romance Series

MacLarens of Fire Mountain

Second Summer, Book One
Hard Landing, Book Two
One More Day, Book Three
All Your Nights, Book Four
Always Love You, Book Five
Hearts Don't Lie, Book Six
No Getting Over You, Book Seven
'Til the Sun Comes Up, Book Eight
Foolish Heart, Book Nine

Macklins of Whiskey Bend

Thorn, Book One
Del, Book Two
Boone, Book Three
Kell, Book four
Zane, Book Four
Josh, Book Five, Coming next in the series!

The Cowboys of Whistle Rock Ranch

The Cowboy's Road Home, Book One
The Cowboy's False Start, Book Two

The Cowboy's Second Chance Family, Book Three, Coming next in the series!

Historical Western Romance Series
Redemption Mountain

Redemption's Edge, Book One
Wildfire Creek, Book Two
Sunrise Ridge, Book Three
Dixie Moon, Book Four
Survivor Pass, Book Five
Promise Trail, Book Six
Deep River, Book Seven
Courage Canyon, Book Eight
Forsaken Falls, Book Nine
Solitude Gorge, Book Ten
Rogue Rapids, Book Eleven
Angel Peak, Book Twelve
Restless Wind, Book Thirteen
Storm Summit, Book Fourteen
Mystery Mesa, Book Fifteen
Thunder Valley, Book Sixteen
A Very Splendor Christmas, Book Seventeen
Paradise Point, Book Eighteen,
Silent Sunset, Book Nineteen
Rocky Basin, Book Twenty
Captive Dawn, Book Twenty-One, Coming Next in the
Series!

MacLarens of Fire Mountain

Tougher than the Rest, Book One
Faster than the Rest, Book Two
Harder than the Rest, Book Three
Stronger than the Rest, Book Four
Deadlier than the Rest, Book Five
Wilder than the Rest, Book Six

MacLarens of Boundary Mountain

Colin's Quest, Book One,
Brodie's Gamble, Book Two
Quinn's Honor, Book Three
Sam's Legacy, Book Four
Heather's Choice, Book Five
Nate's Destiny, Book Six
Blaine's Wager, Book Seven
Fletcher's Pride, Book Eight
Bay's Desire, Book Nine
Cam's Hope, Book Ten

Romantic Suspense

Eternal Brethren, Military Romantic Suspense

Steadfast, Book One
Shattered, Book Two
Haunted, Book Three

Untamed, Book Four
Devoted, Book Five
Faithful, Book Six
Exposed, Book Seven
Undaunted, Book Eight
Resolute, Book Nine
Unspoken, Book Ten
Defiant, Book Eleven

Peregrine Bay, Romantic Suspense

Reclaiming Love, Book One
Our Kind of Love, Book Two

Find all of my books at:
https://www.shirleendavies.com/books.html

About Shirleen

Shirleen Davies writes romance—historical, contemporary, and romantic suspense. She grew up in Southern California, attended Oregon State University, and has degrees from San Diego State University and the University of Maryland. Her real passion is writing emotionally charged stories of flawed people who find redemption through love and acceptance. She now lives with her husband in a beautiful town in northern Arizona.

I love to hear from my readers!

Send me an email: shirleen@shirleendavies.com
Visit my Website: https://www.shirleendavies.com/
Sign up to be notified of New Releases:
https://www.shirleendavies.com/contact/
Follow me on Amazon:
http://www.amazon.com/author/shirleendavies
Follow me on BookBub:
https://www.bookbub.com/authors/shirleen-davies

Other ways to connect with me:

Facebook Author Page:
http://www.facebook.com/shirleendaviesauthor
Pinterest: http://pinterest.com/shirleendavies
Instagram:
https://www.instagram.com/shirleendavies_author/
TikTok: shirleendavies_author
Twitter: www.twitter.com/shirleendavies